Relentless Heart

Relentless Heart

Tyora Moody

Tymm Publishing LLC
Columbia, SC

Relentless Heart
Reed Family Series, Book 3

ISBN-10: 0-9984569-4-2
ISBN-13: 978-0-9984569-4-2

Published by Tymm Publishing LLC
701 Gervais Street, Suite 150-185
Columbia, SC 29201
www.tymmpublishing.com

Cover Design: TywebbinCreations.com
Copy Editing/Proofreading: Felicia Murrell

Chapter 1

Wednesday, November 16 at 12:15 p.m.

The Charlotte-Mecklenburg District Attorney's office could not find sufficient evidence to press charges against Officer Roddy Lane in the officer-related shooting of Danye Lester this past summer. Officer Lane allegedly thought Mr. Lester was reaching for a gun in his pocket. In this life or death situation, due to the fact Mr. Lester ran from the police, Officer Lane made a justifiable decision.

Asia Reed cringed inside as her boss, District Attorney Brandon Lowe read the official statement to the press. She knew the press conference was currently broadcasting live on national news. She turned her head away from the media to look at Brandon, a handsome middle-aged man who definitely liked the cameras. Tall and statuesque,

1

Brandon spoke with an authoritative voice mixed with slight emotion as he acknowledged Danye Lester's family who stood on the other side of the podium.

Asia had to admit she was impressed. Brandon's face had been plastered all over Charlotte during the past election season. Last week, he'd won by a ten-point margin, very different from his landslide four years ago. He'd indicated several times in the past few months, he wanted her to thoroughly comb through every single detail of the eleven-minute ordeal that resulted in Officer Lane fatally shooting twenty-year old Danye. Sometimes she took his edict as a subtle way of telling her he wanted nothing to interfere with his re-election to a second term.

Her team scrutinized the officer shooting case by looking at eyewitness reports and the phone camera footage that went out live on Facebook. She watched every angle they could find of the footage. There were countless testimonies, many supporting how Danye Lester was a good boy in the wrong place at the wrong time. Every time she watched the video, Asia's heart wanted to explode as she saw the young man reach for his pocket. When Danye turned, Officer Lane saw the young man's hand in his pocket and assumed he was reaching for a gun.

There was no gun. Danye laid in a pool of his own blood after being shot twice.

Officer Lane's fourteen-year career as a cop was described by most as exemplary. There were some who wouldn't comment at all. Asia chalked it up to some police code to protect the family in blue. When she shared her final findings with Brandon last Friday, he looked like he didn't know whether to be relieved or worried. He insisted they wait before contacting the family, so she'd spent a tortuous weekend re-examining the footage for what felt like the hundredth time.

There was certainly no relief for her. The investigation was over, but Asia was exhausted. For the first time, she found herself wanting to turn away from a career. Her turmoil stayed hidden except to God. She wasn't a praying woman, but last night she found herself on her knees again asking if justice had truly been served. Seeking justice was what drove her to the profession.

Growing up with her father as a cop, and in later years a police chief, influenced her. It was also a similar shooting incident only a few years ago that led to her father's early retirement. She understood the politics and the public angst, yet time and time again, she was finding justice often escaped the ones who needed it the most. The disappointments were starting to choke her.

Asia took a breath to still her emotions. She turned to observe the downturned mouth of Danye's mother, his uncle and siblings. Her heart broke as she watched tears run down Gloria Lester's face. There would be many more that would not be happy that the investigation didn't lead to a trial. Protests were ongoing all summer and had only quieted a few weeks ago.

She felt in her jacket for her phone. In the midst of the mind-numbing press conference, she was expecting to hear from her sister, Jo any minute now. About three weeks ago, Jo started experiencing labor pains and was rushed to the hospital. Apparently, it was a false alarm, but everyone was on alert for the new baby Reed. It was still a bit early though. Jo had at least another month to go, so all were praying baby girl remained inside her mommy a few weeks longer.

Asia would turn forty in approximately six months. On days like this, when she had to witness the sadness of another mother who lost her son in what seemed like a senseless shooting, she didn't miss motherhood so much. As her sister was near to birthing her second child, in the back of Asia's mind, she pined away that motherhood would never come for her.

Brandon's statement was coming to a close. She recognized the language since she helped write it. Asia blinked as she looked at the span of faces before her. The crowd behind the media had grown since the press conference started at noon.

She turned as Brandon stepped to the side so Gloria Lester could walk towards the microphone to make her statement for the family. Danye's uncle, Sam looked over at her as he held his sister's arm. Asia didn't know how to respond to the anger so she looked away. She noticed Gloria seemed older than her thirty-nine years. Asia swallowed. They were both the same age. Asia had seen a lot of pain, but she'd never experienced Gloria's pain.

Gloria's voice was strong despite her weakened appearance. "I understand the DA's office did a thorough job of looking at all the evidence. My heart still hurts and will never stop hurting from losing my Danye. He would've been twenty-one in a few weeks."

Asia closed her eyes to steel the tears coming. *He was so young.*

She listened as Gloria continued. The woman's shoulders were weighed down with loss, the shadows under her eyes deep and dark from sleepless nights. "I appreciate all of the support. I just want to mourn my boy and remember him. Do know that whatever harm was done whether malicious or not, a person will reap what they sow. Remember that... all of you. You reap what you sow."

You reap what you sow.

Asia frowned as she watched Gloria walk away from the podium. She wasn't a regular church attender, but she was raised at Victory Gospel Church. Sunday School was an every Sunday event. She knew when a case like this was draining her, she needed God. Her mother told her often she should never leave Him out and to always include Him in every aspect of her life.

As the press conference participants dispersed, Asia walked over to Gloria. "Ms. Lester, I'm sorry. We investigated all aspects."

Gloria looked at her, eyes piercing. "I'm sure you did what you thought were all aspects. My son's killer still walks free. Danye wasn't perfect, but he knew better. He wouldn't have resisted arrest. I told him over and over again."

Asia nodded. "I know you did."

"Then this investigation should have turned out differently." Gloria turned away.

Asia took a breath. She looked over to see her boss watching her. With one last glance, she walked inside. As she entered her office, someone called her name from behind. Asia turned.

Brandon came towards her. "You did a good job. I know this wasn't the outcome the family and others wanted to see, but we were fair and we looked at both sides."

Asia didn't have trouble having words when she needed, but right now she felt like words, if any, were trapped in her throat. Thankfully, her office phone rang.

She responded, "I need to get this, Brandon." She sprinted over to the phone hoping it was Jo, her mother or Toni. When she answered, a familiar male voice said, "Hello, Asia." She glanced at her door to see Brandon had left.

"Adam?" She eased herself into her leather chair, feeling the cushions support her. This was a surprising call, so she braced herself.

"Asia. I kind of hate your team decided not to move forward with Officer Lane. It would've been good seeing you in court again."

Asia rolled her eyes. She had dated a good deal of men in her life, but none of them stood out like Adam Locklear. She referred to him as her temporary insanity period. He could be arrogant and overconfident to the point of making one nauseous. But there was also something appealing about him behind the handsome physique. During her time with him, Adam made her laugh and on a few occasions, he'd surprised her with his moments of vulnerability. She'd seen another side of him, or so she thought, until his shiny wrapping wore off.

She responded, "Be glad you were saved. Last I counted, I was way ahead of you on the wins."

Adam laughed. "Counselor, you have become a challenge."

She hated to admit she loved his deep throaty laugh. It was the one thing genuine in the dapper lawyer. Everything else was perfect to a tee. Asia could picture his salt and pepper hair, probably dressed in an Armani suit and soft leather shoes. As a defense attorney, Adam was paid well for defending some of the worst people imaginable.

Asia cleared her throat. "So, what did you really call about? I'm sure you were happy to not have this case go to trial. It would have been hard on everyone involved."

"You're right. It would have been. I was hoping to get together on another matter. Maybe over dinner perhaps?"

Asia felt heat rise on the back of her neck. It'd been three years, and Asia swore to herself she would never go near this man outside a courtroom again. "That's not going to happen. We are strictly to meet on a professional basis. You had your chance remember?"

Adam was silent for a moment.

Now she was concerned. This man was not the silent type. "Adam, are you still there?"

"Yes." Adam's voice sounded strained and seemed to grow lower.

Was there something wrong with the connection? Asia asked, "I can barely hear you, Adam."

He cleared his throat. "Sorry. I was just saying I blew it. I don't have many regrets in life, but you are one of them. I want to help you out with something. I owe you that."

She chuckled, "Help me? What gives you the impression you can help me?" Asia wasn't sure if it was because she already was emotional, but her palms were sweaty.

"I may have some information that interests you. Probably the DA too, but I wanted to run it by you first since I'm pretty sure this will fall on your lap in the near future." Adam paused, "You're the most brilliant counselor I know. You're always going to do the right thing."

Asia leaned back in her chair. If she'd been developing a headache before, now she was starting to feel the pounding. "I'm flattered. Truly. I'm also a little concerned. This information must be pretty serious for you to reach out to me. It's not privileged information, right?"

He laughed, "I'm not trying to get in trouble with the bar."

Despite his laughter, Asia's alarm grew. She'd never seen or heard nervousness radiate from Adam before.

He cleared his throat, "I think it's information you want to be privy to just in case anything goes down. I know you and the world think of me as one of the bad guys, but I have some morals, though most have faded away now."

Asia frowned. "Adam, I don't think I've ever

heard you talk like this before. Is someone going to commit a crime?"

"More like the police may have their eyes on the wrong man. Let's not talk about this on the phone. If you can stand it, I would love to get together this evening. Come by my office. I promise I will keep it professional."

Wrong man? Asia attempted to joke. "You sure this isn't some ploy to get me alone?"

"I adore you, you should know that. I have information you need to know, Asia. Why don't you swing by my office around 7:30 pm?"

Asia's cell phone was beeping. She looked at the screen. Her sister, Toni, was trying to get through. "Okay, Adam, I have to go. It's my sister. I'll meet you tonight at 7:30."

"Thank you, Asia. See you tonight."

She hung up her office phone and grabbed her cell phone. "Hey what's up."

Toni shrieked into the phone. "I'm here with Jo. I just called Bryan and Mom. This is it! No false alarm this time. Baby girl is coming. Get to the hospital as soon as you can."

Asia slapped her forehead. "Okay, okay, I'll be there soon."

She ended the call. For the first time in what

felt like days, a smile broke out on her face, her thoughts on the newborn baby girl she would meet soon. She looked at her desk, which at the moment was a mess of papers and grabbed her coat and purse. On the way out, she stopped by her assistant, Christine Hall's desk.

"Hey, Christine, can you make sure to file the papers on my desk? I'm on my way out. It's official."

Christine beamed. "Jo's having the baby."

"Now as we speak, I'll tell you all about it tomorrow."

"Congratulations!"

"What are congratulations in order for? Are you leaving, Asia?"

Asia turned to look at her boss. "Yes, Jo is in labor right now. You did say last night to take any time I needed. Something up now?"

Brandon shook his head. "No. Go be with your family. You could use the break, Counselor. We'll talk later about what's next."

Asia eyed Brandon for a few seconds. "Thanks, I appreciate you giving me some time to breathe before the next case."

As Asia walked away she remembered Adam mentioning the DA would be interested in knowing the information he had to share. She'd wait to let Brandon know tomorrow after she spoke to Adam.

You reap what you sow.

Asia headed to her black Audi Q5. Gloria Lester's words haunted her, but she didn't know why. Although there was this slight smugness about Officer Lane that got under her skin, she really had turned over every possible angle in the investigation.

As she climbed inside her car, she held out hope that Adam had something to turn around today's events. But attorney-client privilege was serious, Asia didn't see Adam trying to do anything to give up a client.

Why did Adam seem so nervous? Who was this wrong man?

Chapter 2

Wednesday, November 16 at 6:15 p.m.

Asia peered through the glass with her mother in the middle and Toni on the other side. All three were wiping their eyes at the sight of Alisa Jane Powell. It was like getting an early Christmas present. They'd stayed at the hospital all afternoon watching Jo struggle through labor and then give birth. Asia had missed the birth of Jo's oldest child, BJ. Watching baby girl come into the world was a special moment for Asia after a trying day.

The Reed family had two children to spoil now. Asia had already picked up a few things weeks ago for the infant's arrival. She had enjoyed touching the baby clothes before wrapping them.

"She's perfect. I see diva written all over her."

Asia couldn't remember the last time she felt this kind of pure joy.

Toni snorted, "Uh, she is not going to be like her auntie Asia."

Asia smirked, "Why not? She's wearing that pink onesie. We need another fashionable girl in the family. Jo is not a girlie girl."

"What you trying to say about me?"

Asia glanced at her baby sister's long poncho shirt over animal print leggings. "I like your boots."

"Whatever. You're not the only fashion-conscience Reed. You just have the bigger paycheck."

Vanessa shook her head. "Enough, you two. I'm grateful to have another grandchild. Oh, sweet little Alisa, we're going to have so much fun."

Toni shook her head. "That is going to be one spoiled little girl."

Asia's phone rang. She reached into her pocketbook and looked at her phone, hoping she hadn't lost track of time. A quick glance at the phone told her she still had another hour before meeting Adam.

Who was this? The phone number looked vaguely familiar.

"Are you going to answer that or what?" Her mother looked at her annoyed.

"I'm trying to figure out who it is."

"Girl, try answering it," Toni shook her head.

Asia rolled her eyes and turned away from her mother and sister. "Hello?"

"Finally, someone from the Reed family answered, although I wasn't expecting it would be you."

Asia stopped in her tracks, recognizing the deep voice on the other end. "Jax. Well, it's good to hear from you..." She sighed, "bro."

"What? Asia Reed acknowledging me as a brother. Who knew a new niece would make this stunning change in you? How is the newborn? Anyone going to send me photos?"

"Why aren't you here? You are a part of this family, aren't you? I mean when's the last time we've seen you?"

"You miss me? This is really touching coming from you, Asia."

Asia gripped the phone. "Whatever, Jax."

"And there is my older sister. For a minute, I didn't recognize you. You got a minute to tell me about Jo and Bryan's latest addition?"

"How about I get Toni to snap a photo and text you, okay?"

"Whoa...wait, before you try getting rid of me. I need to talk to you and Jo at some point. Soon. Probably when I'm in Charlotte."

Adam, now Jax. What's up with all these people wanting to talk?

She frowned. "What's this about?"

"I want to talk to you both in person. Let Vanessa know I'll be there for Thanksgiving next week, if she doesn't mind adding an extra chair."

"This is different for you."

"Vanessa invited me. And I'd kind of like to be around family for a change." He paused, "It's been different with Mom gone. Anyway, I'll be looking for that photo of my new niece. Good talking to you, Asia. I hope you know we're on the same side."

The same side. Yeah, right.

She had no problem admitting she'd not come to terms that her and Jax were related. A possible reason could've been the way she found out. As a little girl, she'd been out with her dad when a strange woman came up to them. Jo was home with their mother. As Asia watched her dad have words with the woman, she'd noticed a little boy about the size of Jo looking at her. All the way home, she'd asked her dad, "Who was that woman? Whose little boy?"

Later that night at dinner, she'd asked her father again. By the look on her mother's face, Asia knew her questions had sparked a fire that continued to burn for years afterwards. At the age of six, she'd already started recognizing and questioning bad behavior.

Asia peered at her mom as she approached. She took a breath before asking, "So you invited Jax to Thanksgiving?"

Vanessa turned around. "I have invited him to all of our family get togethers every year, especially since his mom died. It's been two years, you know? His mother had no family as she was an only child. He's alone and he's your brother. Was that him on the phone? I didn't hear yelling. Are you two getting along?"

Asia scoffed. "I happened to be the one Reed who picked up the phone. I'm sure I was his last resort."

Toni exclaimed, "Oh, that was him? He just texted me. I'm going to send him back a few photos of Alisa."

Asia sighed. Her younger siblings, including Jo,

adored Jax. That always baffled her. "Good, that's what he wanted...along with some other things, I guess."

Vanessa frowned. "What did he say?"

"He's coming for Thanksgiving so you can put out an extra chair. His words, not mine. He also wants to speak to me and Jo about something. I wonder what our half-brother has to share with us."

"Asia, you're almost in your forties. At some point, you need to accept Jax is your brother. He didn't come from me, but he's your blood."

Asia shook her head. "I still don't know how you just accepted him."

Her mother stared at her before sighing. "I didn't for a very long time. Especially when his mom was alive. That woman gave me fits. I'm sorry it took me so long because I feel like you soaked up all my negativity and directed it towards Jax."

"No, I didn't. He's arrogant. Whether he was my brother or not, I'd have issues with him."

Vanessa shook her head. "You two are more alike than you know. He's the way he is because he's been left out. His mother wanted your dad to be a part of his life, but she didn't want us in it. If she had her way, she'd prefer your dad left us all behind."

"I know. She was an evil woman. You don't think Jax doesn't have any of that in him?"

"Asia, we all have our not so nice sides. Nobody is all good. Jax wants and has always wanted a family. You know when his mother was getting chemo treatments in this same hospital, she didn't have anyone to bring her back and forth. Jax couldn't keep driving from Atlanta. Guess who chauffeured her?"

Asia frowned, "Are you serious? I didn't know you did that."

"When you profess Jesus Christ as Lord, you can't choose who you forgive. God forgives us. When God places something in your heart to do, you can either do it or not."

"You decided it was better to do it?"

Her mother nodded, "I needed to do it. Before that woman left this world, we needed to have a long talk. She asked me to look after Jax."

Asia scoffed. "The nerve."

Her mother touched her shoulder, "Jax didn't ask to be here. He only has his dad ...and us. You're both valuable to each other more than you know. Learn to love each other. You've been closer to people who you don't even share blood with, so why not give him a chance? There is nothing for you to lose."

Asia thought about Adam for some reason. She'd let herself get close to him. He really was the most arrogant person she'd ever met. She'd enjoyed their almost seven months together, until it went downhill.

"I need to go meet with someone."

Vanessa raised her eyebrow. "Now? Certainly not a date. I thought you were too busy for dating these days."

"It's not a date, but... Momma, are you throwing shade?"

Her mother threw up her hands. "What does that even mean? Look, all I know is your most consistent relationship is with your work. And that phone stays glued to your hand."

Asia looked down at her phone which she hadn't returned to her pocketbook. "Funny. True, but funny. I'll see you later. Tell Jo to get some rest. That cutie in there is probably going to snatch all her beauty sleep."

Asia marched down the hall, her heels tapping on the floor. The fact that she was meeting with

Adam Locklear meant she did have the capacity to forgive.

As she rode down the hospital elevator, she thought about the time she entered Adam's office to surprise him. The surprise was on her when she saw his assistant straddled across him in a chair. Needless to say, their whirlwind of romantic evenings became a distant memory.

Then again, maybe she really didn't forgive him. More like over the past three years, she'd asserted her own sweet revenge. Asia relished her court victories against Adam. That she did well. Every single time. Adam Locklear was a very good defense attorney.

She was a better prosecutor. The best.

Asia didn't let much, if anything slip by her. She was reminded of Adam's nervousness on the phone. Adam liked to win, so she needed to learn what had brought about the urgency she sensed earlier. Whatever the repercussions, she wanted to be on top of it now. After today, she needed justice to prevail.

Chapter 3

Wednesday, November 16 at 7:13 p.m.

The night air had dipped rapidly into the fifties. Her suede blazer felt fine earlier, but now she could feel the chilly air slicing through to the short sleeve shirt she wore underneath. Asia clicked the button on her key fob to unlock the car door and start the engine. As she climbed in, the smooth sounds of Gregory Porter pulsated from the speakers. She sat for a minute, knowing she needed to get moving if she wanted to get to Adam's office in time.

Today, she'd seen one mother's agony of receiving no justice for her son. Her sister's pain and joy delivering a beautiful baby girl. Her own mother's peaceful face and complete acceptance of a man, born out of an affair years ago. She had no idea her mother had been inviting Jax to join the family for Thanksgiving or any event. She really just thought he showed up when he wanted to as a reminder of his existence. Jax lived in Atlanta, separated by a four-hour drive, yet he rarely came to Charlotte. He seemed to stop coming after his mom died. Maybe too many memories. Asia hated to admit she was curious why he would come this year.

He's alone. He's your brother.

"Okay, that's enough of this," she thought out loud. She hated her emotions being all over the place. She didn't like it, not one bit. It felt like a bubble was growing bigger and bigger inside of her until she would explode. Losing it meant she wasn't in control. She had to be in control which was why she needed to get to Adam and find out what he knew.

His timing after the press conference today was rather ominous.

She still secretly hoped it had to do with Danye Lester. *Is that wrong of me?* Asia truly hunted for any piece of evidence to build a case against Office Roddy Lane. She wanted the slain young man to not become yet another victim of no justice received. But she couldn't, not inside the confines of the law. Coasting along the expressway, she tried humming to the song to keep her thoughts from the looming failure she'd conjured in her mind.

Asia's mind shifted back to Adam, not about what information he'd have for her in a few minutes, but their short-lived romance. Adam was definitely not husband material. Plus, he'd been married once and had two kids. The divorce was brutal. It wasn't long after he officially divorced that he started dating Asia. She used to tease him, saying she was rebound material, but he'd promised he was over his wife. Asia almost believed him. Right up until she found him with his legal assistant, Candie Parker. Asia liked to think she would've connected the dots sooner if she hadn't been so love-struck. Candie was beautiful. How could a man resist someone like her being in his office day in and day out?

"We would've made some pretty children though," she said out loud. Then she laughed at herself. It had indeed been a long day for her to ponder these desperate thoughts. She would listen to what Adam had to tell her and take the information back to her boss in the morning. She'd made many mistakes, and now she was just too old and too tired to be making anymore. Asia had been celibate the past three years thanks to Adam. She intended to keep it that way.

Asia took the downtown exit towards Adam's office. She passed the tower and turned into the adjacent parking garage. She nodded at the nightshift guard, an older African American man who'd been there a long time. He recognized her, smiled, and then lifted the gate for her to drive into the garage. Adam's office was on the fifth floor so she circled the parking garage, finding an empty spot close to the entrance door.

She grabbed her purse off the seat and glanced around as she stepped out of her car. There were only a few cars. Adam's white Mercedes beamed against the wall near the entrance. She wasn't a fan of being in a parking garage this late. Her heels tapped sharply as she quickly made her way towards the doors ahead. Once inside the building entrance from the garage, she pressed the elevator. A humming noise, like a nearby generator, filled the foyer where she stood. Its loudness gave her the creeps.

She leaped inside as soon as the elevator doors opened and stabbed the number five. Her heart was beating as she thought about her earlier conversation with Adam.

Just in case anything goes down.

She had a feeling sleep wouldn't elude her again tonight. Asia couldn't remember the last time she'd felt this exhausted. Strangely, she felt wired too as though she'd gulped down a large cup of strong black coffee. She watched the numbers rise on the elevator, wondering if this was even a good idea. Maybe she should've told Adam she'd meet him in the morning when she was rested and fresh.

As soon as the elevator doors opened, she looked out into the hallway. Only when the doors started to close did she jump forward with her body. She leaped into the hallway, and the door shut behind her.

It was quiet in the hallway, which shouldn't have been out of the ordinary since it was after hours. Adam's law office was on one side with another set of offices on the opposite side. She turned to look at the double doors to her right. The office was dark and the colored title on the door said, Advantage Data Systems. She didn't remember that company being there before.

She turned back to the left and approached the double glass doors of Locklear Law Firm. Asia took a deep breath and held her knuckles up to knock, but then decided to pull on one of the doors. This was a professional visit. Like old times, the door swung open. Past history, Adam would leave the door open for her.

She stepped inside. The Locklear Law Firm was a sleek set of offices fitted with modern furniture, not at all like the traditional look and feel of her state-owned office building.

She called out, "Adam?"

His office was probably less than ten yards away directly to her left. She expected him to step out like he usually would. His thick hair would tell her what kind of day he'd had. If it was smoothed back, he'd obviously had a big win that day. If his salt and pepper mane was tousled, Adam had spent most of the day about to pull his hair out over a case. He didn't like when things were messy, but he enjoyed the challenge.

That was the other thing she liked about him. He presented this persona in the courtroom and with clients, but she'd seen his "real" human side.

Asia frowned. Maybe he was on the phone. As she moved closer towards his office, she would have heard his booming voice. He wasn't the kind of person with an inside voice.

Something was wrong. It was way too quiet. Adam expected her so he wouldn't have stepped out.

Before she stepped inside Adam's door, her senses heightened. There was a metallic smell in the air. She gripped her bag and compelled her legs to move inside Adam's office. There were two lamps on, one on the desk and a tall lamp in the back corner across from his desk. She could see the buildings across the street through the two large windowpanes on either side of the desk.

Whether her mind was preparing her for the scene, she didn't know, but her eyes focused on Adam's thick hair first. It was tousled. Then she saw his face. She stared in disbelief as her already wearied brain tried to process. Somewhere she heard a screeching noise.

It was coming from her. She was screaming.

Her eyes watered as she observed the blood-spattered wall behind Adam's desk. His head was leaned back against his beloved black leather chair, eyes vacant.

She covered her mouth and stumbled backwards. Tears ran down her eyes as she fumbled for her phone. She had to get help.

Oh, Adam. What happened? Who did this?

Chapter 4

Wednesday, November 16 at 9:02 p.m.

Asia answered questions from the officers after they arrived. They knew who she was. Most cops did because her dad was the former chief of police. Most cops in the department watched her and her siblings grow up, and in the past few years, many law enforcement were called in by her to sit on the witness stand. She knew the routine and told the attending officers, she would sit in the coffee shop downstairs.

She was surprised she remembered it. When she first started meeting Adam, it's where they met in the evenings. The first time they met, Adam saw the writing on the wall and laid out a possible deal for his client. Asia tended to not do deals unless the defendant had something to offer in another case. She'd told him she would think about it overnight, but instead of leaving, she sat for another hour indulging in a slice of strawberry shortcake. She was surprised to learn the super fit defense attorney had a sweet tooth he struggled with like she did. After that, they gradually started going to dinner, attending events and hanging out on the weekend. She'd shoved her history with Adam to the back corners of her mind.

Now sitting in the same booth they sat in years ago, Asia sipped coffee. She kept thinking to herself, what if she'd left the hospital sooner. How ironic she was running late and not really caring about punctuality.

Would she have passed Adam's killer? Would she still be alive now?

She jumped when she saw a shadow pass by her on the right. Asia looked up to see a man. He was actually quite handsome, though she couldn't tell his ethnicity. He could be a very light-skinned black man or Hispanic.

He held out a badge, "Detective Isaac Coleman. I'm with homicide. You found Adam Locklear?"

She nodded. "I'm Asia Reed."

Detective Coleman nodded, "Yes, I know. You're an assistant district attorney."

"You've done your homework."

"I'm sorry. I know all of this must be a huge shock. Do you mind if I sit down?"

"Sure."

The detective slid into the booth in front of her. His eyes were warm and friendly. She was surprised she hadn't met him before. Asia headed up the District Attorney Homicide Team and worked with most of the homicide detectives in Charlotte Mecklenburg Police Department.

Asia took a breath. "I have had quite the day you know. I led the team who delivered bad news to Danye Lester's family this morning. Though I'm sure Officer Lane and his family are elated. My sister had a baby girl. I'm an aunt again." Her voice shook, "Now this."

Detective Coleman lifted his eyebrow. "Wow, you have had quite the day. Here I thought my day was bad. I've had a few cases trickle in over the past few weeks, but I have a feeling this will be my first big case."

Asia sat up. The coffee was helping her senses. "I thought you were new. Your instincts are right. Adam Locklear is ... was a big-time attorney. He had a very interesting clientele. I can promise you, the DA is going to be all over this, if not already, definitely in the morning."

Detective Coleman smiled. "Hey, I'm up for the challenge. I moved up to being a detective a few weeks ago. My partner is Detective Barry Lamb."

"Ole Barry is your partner?" Asia shook her head. "He's close to retirement. Kind of a curmudgeon too. So, he sent you down here to interview me? Figures. He doesn't like me, mainly because I'm a Reed."

Detective Coleman cleared his throat and gave a slight grin. "That makes two of us. He doesn't like me either. He's not here. A family thing going on."

Asia narrowed her eyes. "Really? He's letting you, no offense, a rookie, take this on yourself?"

Coleman's mouth twitched, but he didn't respond.

Asia held up her hands. "Like I said, no offense. You should know your partner wasn't a fan of Adam. A jury found a guy not guilty, Ethan Consentino who Lamb worked really hard to arrest for murder. Adam claimed your partner planted the murder weapon. That wasn't my case, but I remember the DA being so upset because it was a pretty critical piece of evidence. It really messed up the credibility of the case. Ethan walked, might still be walking around."

Coleman nodded, "So you're saying my partner isn't going to miss Mr. Locklear?"

"Truth be told, Adam won't be missed by a lot of people. My sister wasn't a fan of his either."

"Your sister, she was a detective?"

Asia nodded. "Yeah, Detective Jo Reed-Powell. We didn't get to work together often, but about a year ago we both worked the Jeffrey Maddock case. She took some time off to make a baby."

"She's the sister who delivered tonight?"

"Yep."

"You have children?"

Odd question. Or maybe just a sore point for her. Asia shook her head. "I'm married to my work. I enjoy being an auntie though."

Detective Coleman cleared his throat.

Seeing his discomfort, Asia spoke. "I appreciate the small talk, Detective Coleman. You want to know why I was at Adam Locklear's office, right?"

He flipped his notepad. "I'm sorry. I wanted to give you some time."

Asia looked at him and smiled. "You're going to be a great detective." She leaned back in the booth. "Mr. Locklear called me earlier today. He said he had some information to tell me. I assumed it was from one of his clients. He didn't want to talk on the phone and felt it was best to meet in person. Locklear was one of the best defense attorneys money could buy, but in recent years, he hadn't won a case against me."

"Really?"

Asia nodded. "He was good. He didn't like to lose. For him to share information with me, it must have been big. I also sensed he was apprehensive. So I agreed to meet with him even though it'd been a long day. I didn't know someone else would be meeting with him first."

They sat in silence for a minute.

Asia continued, "The night shift guard let me through the garage. Maybe there was someone before me. I'm sure cameras are in various areas of the building. Your team is looking into who entered the building?"

He nodded. "Yes, we're gathering all footage. The office door was not locked as you know. I guess because Mr. Locklear was expecting you." Detective Coleman, flipped through his notes. "He didn't have anything on his assistant's calendar that I could see about your meeting."

Asia frowned. "He didn't tell his assistant I was

coming? That's weird. He had to tell her to leave the door unlocked. Maybe the meeting was at the last minute and he just forgot. He'd probably have our meeting on his phone though. He was a fanatic about his phone."

Her mind drifted to the past, recalling how Adam would get lost in his email as they sat over coffee. She didn't mind at the time, she did the same thing.

Coleman interrupted her memories. "Did you go to his office often? I mean you're a prosecutor and he's a defense attorney."

Asia thought for a moment before answering. It probably appeared strange that she would know Adam's habits about his phone and calendar. She sighed. It was best to be transparent so Coleman knew her history with Adam. "We met outside the courtroom on friendly terms for a few months. This was years ago."

"You dated?"

Asia's face grew warm again. *Why did she feel embarrassed?* She shrugged. "Let's just say Adam Locklear can be... I should say he was charming when he wanted to be."

"But he still made enemies?"

"He defended some of the worst criminals. Believe me, your partner will give you an earful."

"I can't wait. Since he wanted to see you, could this be one of the cases you prosecuted?"

"Could be a new or old case, I'm not sure. Anyone I prosecuted should currently be serving prison time. If someone has had an early release, I would think they would be trying to get their life back. He did say the police had the wrong man." She paused, thinking she needed to stop rambling. Asia struggled to replay the phone conversation in her head. "I wish I knew what he meant."

The detective leaned forward. "You said wrong man? Did he drop any other hints?"

She focused her eyes on Coleman's face. The detective had large, warm brown eyes, and he appeared very concerned. Asia blinked to refocus. "Adam hinted that he needed to pass information to me just in case anything went down."

"Like his murder? He knew he had information that could get him killed." Detective Coleman frowned, "Do you think maybe you should be careful?"

Asia shook her head. "He didn't say that exactly."

"But you don't know what he was going to tell you."

She twisted her fingers. This was not what she needed. "No. He did say he reached out to a client." *Or did he say that? Adam said he wasn't trying to do anything to get disbarred. But he was nervous.*

Pressure was slowly building around her temples making her eyes water. She took a breath. "I'm really worn out. Can we touch base and compare notes tomorrow? The coffee is wearing off and I don't have it in me. There's nothing more I know to share. I need a night's sleep."

"Sure. I'm sorry." Coleman climbed out of the booth and held out his hand.

Asia grabbed her empty coffee cup. Surprised, but too tired to ignore the gesture, she grabbed his hand as he helped her rise from the booth. The detective was strong. "Thank you, you're quite the gentleman."

She wasn't too tired to notice they were the exact same height.

"You know I just thought of something. I've never met them, but Adam has an ex-wife and kids. I want to say he had a boy and girl. They live in Florida. Someone needs to tell them."

"Of course. We will contact the family. I'm sorry

about your loss. Tonight can't be easy. I will be in touch tomorrow, Ms. Reed."

"Thank you. You have a good evening, Detective Coleman. I hope you're enjoying your career as a detective. These cases can wear you down."

"I'm good so far. I'll be even better when we catch this killer."

Asia smiled as she walked away. She liked his ambition. This early in his career, he just received one of those cases that would keep an investigator up all night.

Tomorrow she would get answers, but now she just needed to get home.

Asia didn't indulge in alcohol too often, but she was ready for a much-needed glass of Moscato. She didn't know who else would grieve for Adam, but she had a feeling a few tears would be shed by her tonight.

Chapter 5

Thursday, November 17 at 2:20 p.m.

Asia blew out a breath and leaned back in her leather chair. She was tired. More than just not getting any sleep last night, she was worn out from looking through cases she'd prosecuted with Adam as defense counsel. All she could think about was Adam's words to her on the phone.

Wrong man. Who did he mean? If she feared anything, it would be prosecuting an innocent person.

She looked up to see her assistant, Christine, plop down in the chair in front of Asia's desk. "It's such a shame, Ms. Reed, that Mr. Locklear couldn't have just talked to you on the phone. Why do you think he wanted to wait?"

Asia shook her head. "I have no idea. I do know

anytime someone doesn't trust talking on the phone, the information must be extremely sensitive." She glanced at the clock on her office wall. "You need to take a break and I definitely need a break. Go grab some lunch. When you get back, you can look through the rest of this list. I will probably head over and see if the detectives came across anything in Locklear's office."

"I hope they have some leads for you." Christine pushed her blue eyeglass frames up higher on her nose. "Don't forget to eat something yourself, Ms. Reed. You're living off coffee today. Would you like me to bring you some food back?"

"No, I'm good."

She watched Christine close the office door.

I'm really not good.

She was too frustrated to worry about hunger. Asia ran her hands across her hair. Despite her stress, every hair was smoothly in place. She ran her fingers down her long ponytail and pulled it around to hang across her shoulder. She glanced down at her legal pad where she'd listed her cases. There were so many scenarios surrounding why someone would walk into Adam's office and kill him.

Someone could have been nursing a grudge

against Adam for keeping a criminal out of jail that she failed to prosecute. The problem with that scenario is there were none. Adam never won a case against her.

If it was someone she convicted, they were sitting in jail. Unless it was someone recently released. But why would they go after Adam instead of her?

Asia's head began to pound. She didn't like the direction of her thoughts. She leaned across the desk and placed her face in her hands. Adam didn't want to talk on the phone. If he called her, it had to be information about one of her cases or a case the DA's office prosecuted.

How in the world am I supposed to read the mind of a dead man?

If only Adam had left some type of clue.

She closed her eyes and lifted her face towards the ceiling. Asia didn't pray often, but she knew God knew what happened in Adam's office last night.

Lord, can you show me something? I'm a little lost here, and I know I can admit this to you. I'm afraid. You know I try to do the right thing. I could use your protection. A little direction would be great too.

Her eyes snapped open. She looked down at the

legal pad again. While she was not the most devout person, Asia took her faith seriously. She wasn't expecting to see a name written in front of her glow on the page like some special effect in a movie. If only it could be that easy.

Someone knocked on her office door. Asia jumped, her heart racing. She rubbed her hands across her chest as though she could slow her heart. "Come in."

When she saw Brandon at the door, she leaned back in her chair, trying to appear as if she wasn't slowly freaking out. "Boss, what can I do for you?"

He stepped into her office. "I think I should be asking you that question."

She frowned. Brandon wasn't one to come walking to your office. He liked to summon people to his office. "I don't understand."

His eyes grew wide. "You witnessed a horrible crime. Against a...friend. Should you be in the office today? It's not like you ever take any time off. Enjoy your sister's little one."

Asia narrowed her eyes. Her boss was not the touchy feely type of guy, but he was one of a very few people besides her family who knew she dated Adam. And he only knew because he and his wife ran into her with Adam at a restaurant. Up until that night, they'd kept their relationship discreet.

She stood from her desk. "I'm fine. We had a brief relationship three years ago. History. Adam was a colleague as he was also to you."

Brandon forced a laugh. "Glad you came to your senses. And there was no friendship between me and Adam Locklear. I was in the majority that didn't like him. May he rest in peace." He looked at the pile of folders on her desk. "If you don't mind me asking why were you at Adam's office?"

"How did you know I was there?"

Brandon raised his eyebrow. "Captain called this morning. He wanted to know if you were alright. My surprise because I had no clue what happened last night. I mean I heard about Adam's shooting on the news, but I didn't know you found him. That was kept out of the news."

Asia nodded. "I'm thankful. I'm sure the DA's office didn't need that kind of publicity. We're still being raked over the coals for our decision to not investigate Officer Lane."

Brandon frowned. "Yes, that's true. Were you still friends?"

"We had a mutual respect for being on opposite

sides." She sighed and crossed her arms. "Adam had information he wanted to share."

Brandon seemed to freeze in place. "What kind of information?"

"The kind he will never be able to tell me himself unless he decides to haunt me from wherever his poor soul has gone."

Both of Brandon's eyebrows shot up. He stared at her desk again. "You don't think this information had anything to do with his death?"

"He called me to let me know he had information I needed to know. I went to meet him last night and found him with a hole in his head. I don't know what to think, Brandon."

Brandon let out a long breath, "This is disturbing, Asia. You know I don't believe in coincidences."

Asia leaned against her desk. "I don't either. Whatever information Adam had, he mentioned something about having the wrong man."

Brandon crossed his arms and observed her. "For what case?"

She walked backed behind her desk. "Good question. I'm going to see Detective Coleman to see what he's found out so far."

"Detective Coleman?" Brandon frowned. "Homicide?"

Asia nodded. "He's new, but his partner is Detective Lamb. I expect more from Coleman. You know Lamb had a chip on his shoulder since Adam's client, Ethan Consentino, was found not guilty by the jury."

Brandon nodded. "I remember. You know there has to be a mile-long list of people who would stand in line to pull the trigger. Adam was ruthless in the courtroom and very well paid. Be sure you start with the grudges. Those who may have openly threatened Locklear."

She leaned over her desk and picked up her legal pad. "Christine and I have started several lists. Adam didn't win any cases against me, but he also didn't specify it was one of my cases. I'm just assuming."

She looked down at the empty coffee cup on her desk and realized she should've taken Christine's offer for lunch. Her body felt weak all of a sudden, though she couldn't blame her feeling on lack of food. "I need to go grab some lunch and head to the precinct."

Brandon pointed to her. "Keep me updated and be careful. We need to find out this information

Adam wanted to share. Better to be ahead and not caught off guard later."

"I know. Will do." She watched him walk out before grabbing her bag. Brandon was too much of a gentleman, but she knew the politician side of him would never admit this was making him nervous too.

Asia picked up her phone and dialed. "Yes, may I speak to Detective Coleman, please?"

She hoped the rookie detective got a lot further along than she did today.

Chapter 6

Thursday, November 17 at 3:13 pm

Asia slurped the rest of her iced tea and took a breath before throwing the cup in the trashcan outside the precinct. Nourishment was what she needed. It also helped that the temperatures were low 60s and the sun was shining. For about an hour, she'd escaped her inner turmoil. Now she had to head back into reality as she entered the building.

In homicide, the Locklear investigation was front and center. Detective Coleman stood surrounded by his partner, Detective Lamb, two other detectives from their unit and Sgt. Elaine Maddison. It was good to see Elaine as a new addition to the force. Asia had noticed without her sister on the force it looked like an all-male club.

She'd missed seeing Jo here at the precinct. Her sister was one of the best detectives.

She sauntered over, "Sgt. Maddison, I hope you've solved the case with all these heads around the evidence board."

Maddison was shorter than Asia, but her muscular stature was intimidating. She wore her long blond hair, now with gray streaks, in a ponytail piled on top of her head. The sergeant, though a woman, could be described as handsome. She granted Asia a tight smile, "Ah, just in time, Ms. Reed. We've been expecting you."

Two of the detectives dispersed as if they had more important things to do. Asia acknowledged Detective Coleman who returned a slight nod. She turned her attention to Detective Lamb who seemed to keep a permanent scowl on his face.

"So, bring me up to speed. The DA's very interested in finding out leads, especially since Adam had information that pertained to the DA's office. Any persons-of-interest yet?"

"Besides you?" Detective Lamb cracked.

Asia stared at him. "Excuse me?"

Sgt. Maddison cleared her throat. "Detective Lamb is being his usual charming self. Of course, you're not a suspect. We appreciate your cooperation last night and as you probably know, we were able to keep your name out of the media."

"Uh huh. Yes, I noticed that. Thank you." Asia kept her eyes on Lamb. "I see where you're going with this though. I'm the one who found him. I'm the one whom he had something to tell. The problem is if I killed him, I did it in vain. I'm still clueless as to what he had to tell me. Don't you think I should've at least gotten my information first?"

Lamb spat, "Maybe you did and you didn't like what he had to say."

Asia narrowed her eyes. "What's your problem? As I recall, you hated the man. I would say you have more motive than anyone in this room."

Detective Lamb uncrossed his arms and took a step forward.

The sergeant frowned, "That's enough, Detective Lamb. If the DA gave the okay for Ms. Reed to join us in the investigation, he has faith in her. Besides, any case where she served as prosecutor could help us narrow down a suspects list. You said the only clue Locklear gave you was you had the wrong man. For what case?"

Asia eyed Lamb for a few seconds before she shrugged. "I've started a list, but we don't know if it's about any of my cases. We're only assuming because Adam reached out to me. Right now, I just finished up an investigation. I'm pretty sure it's not a past case."

Lamb stated, "Because you would never put an innocent man away. That's never happened before."

The older detective had started to exhaust her patience. "You know how this works, Lamb. You guys present a case to us on why a person should be charged and placed on trial. You collect the evidence."

Lamb's face grew red.

Asia wasn't trying to throw a jab at him about his past discretion, but he'd asked for it. She continued, "I'm hoping we can find out who Locklear talked to prior to last night. Somebody knew exactly where to find him."

Detective Coleman, who'd been quiet finally spoke up. "We were able to touch base with his legal assistant this morning. She will be coming in soon so we can interview her. We've been able to piece together some of his activities the last few weeks from her calendar."

Asia crossed her arms. "Good, some real detective work is going on." She snapped at Lamb.

"Do you mind us getting down to business now, Detective Lamb, or are you still having thoughts on making this easy to pin on me?"

Lamb stared at her for a moment. "Rookie, here's got it. I need a refill." Lamb grabbed his coffee cup off the desk and walked off.

Asia knew Lamb hated Locklear, but he was still obligated to do his job. He flat-out didn't like her because she was a Reed. Jo had complained about run-ins with Lamb too. It all went back to the Ethan Consentino incident which rippled throughout the police force, digging at the credibility of everyone. She hadn't been assigned to the case, but if she had, Asia would have caught the fact that the crime scene had been compromised. It was those details that a good defense attorney like Locklear relished in finding.

Asia could still remember her dad's, then police chief, anger with Lamb. He suspended Lamb without pay.

What in the world was Lamb thinking trying to throw my name in the ring as a suspect?

She turned her attention to Detective Coleman who was observing her. His eyes were warm and seemed concerned. "Sorry about my partner, Ms.

Reed. Would you like to take a look at what we've found so far?"

"I would. But I have a question." She turned to Sgt. Madison. "Why was Coleman the only one on the scene last night? Is there anything I should be concerned about here, Sergeant?"

Sgt. Madison's blue eyes were definitely not warm, but she responded with a civil tone, "Lamb was pulled away on another matter, but he's up-to-speed now. I have confidence in Coleman. He's got a good head start. You were very helpful last night despite the scene you had to witness. My condolences, by the way."

She nodded. Asia decided to let her concerns about Lamb slide for the time being. Especially since everyone now knew about her brief relationship with Adam. She had no intention of letting their knowledge stop her. Everyone did things they later regretted. Learn from the mistakes and keep it moving had always been her motto.

"Detective, please show me what you have."

"So, it appears in the days prior to his death, Locklear met with several clients as would be normal for his practice." Coleman pointed to the board. "Yesterday he met with Officer Roddy Lane.

That was mainly to be with Officer Lane and his family during the press conference held by the DA's office."

The man's voice was soothing and calm. Coleman glided his hand down the board, "To go back further this week, around 4:00 pm on Monday he met with Lawrence Warren, a real estate broker who'd been accused of killing his wife."

Asia thought the name was familiar. "I vaguely remember seeing that on the news a few weeks back. Who was involved with that investigation?"

Sgt. Madison pointed. "Well, Coleman can bring you up to speed. The Warren case was one of his first cases."

Coleman nodded. "Yes. Mrs. Janice Warren filed for a divorce. Witnesses in that case point to the fact that the marriage had grown ugly and emotions had escalated. We're still building the case, but Mr. Warren probably offed his wife to avoid paying alimony."

Asia nodded. "Sounds like Adam's kind of case. I'm sure he would've found some way to make Mr. Warren appear innocent."

"You're probably right, but it also sounds like he would've had a hard time if you were the prosecutor." Coleman smiled before turning back towards the evidence board.

Asia felt her face grow warm. Coleman was definitely attentive last night as he listened to her. *He didn't miss a thing I said.*

He continued, "So now on Tuesday morning, Locklear spent time in court with Jack Camden for his bond hearing at 10 am. Camden was arrested Monday evening for domestic abuse charges against his wife."

Asia shook her head. "Locklear never had a dull case. Jack Camden, isn't he on the city council?"

Coleman cracked a smile again. "He is. You're very well-informed. I'm impressed."

She returned his smile. "I make it my business to know who's who in this city."

Coleman looked back at the board. "The week prior, he met with two other clients who have trial dates in the future. One was a vehicular homicide and the other was an assault case."

Asia crossed her arms. "I don't know about these open cases. We're creeping into attorney-client privilege. He wouldn't share any information. The motive to kill Locklear can be endless. For all we know, Locklear's death may have nothing to do with any of my cases or the information he wanted to share. Like I said, I don't know what he meant by having the wrong man."

Sgt. Madison threw up her hands. "I'm feeling your frustration. We need answers soon. Locklear was well-known in Charlotte. Even the mayor called this morning inquiring about the investigation. Apparently, they were friends."

Asia scoffed. "Figures."

Madison winked. "I will leave you two to this. Keep up the good work, Coleman."

Asia crossed her arms and leaned against the desk as the sergeant walked away. She looked at Coleman who seemed stunned by his superior's compliment.

Her eyes were drawn to his face and for a few seconds they just stared at each other before she asked, "Do you have camera footage from last night? Surely you saw who came in and out of the building last night."

A slow grin stretched across Detective Coleman's face. "That's what I have for you next. We have the killer on the screen."

She frowned, "Really? Is this going to be simpler than I thought?"

"Maybe. Maybe not." She followed him over to a desk across from the evidence board.

As Isaac sat down, Asia's eyes were drawn to the detective's hands. There was no wedding ring, not that that should've been her concern at the moment. She guessed he must have been close to her age or younger. Despite being a new detective, he seemed very comfortable in his role. He certainly was on top of things compared to his veteran partner.

Coleman double-clicked on an icon on the computer screen and a video player displayed. He pressed play. The camera displayed the area outside the office across from the elevator. Isaac explained, "I have logged who arrived on the elevator and ..." He clicked. "There's also a camera in front of the office area. Basically, cameras were installed at all the entry and exit doors in the building."

Asia nodded. "I was wondering if a camera would be in his office. That would get tricky trying to protect sensitive information from clients."

"You're right. We only have the advantage of seeing who entered the law firm, not necessarily his office. I'm not sure how promising these are as leads. I have to warn you some identifying is still to come."

"Nothing is ever easy, detective." Asia leaned in

closer to the monitor. Her eyes were on the screen, but she had to force her mind to focus. Coleman's cologne matched his personality, manly, but not overpowering. Just subtle enough to entice her attention. She'd only been around this man twice in the last twenty-four hours and instead of focusing on her ex-boyfriend's murder, she was wondering about Coleman's cologne brand.

Maybe she was too close. Too close to this case and...

Asia focused on where Isaac was pointing towards the screen.

"You see his assistant left at 6:54 pm. Locklear was the only one in the office."

Asia caught her breath as she recognized Adam's assistant. She'd only seen this woman a few times. Candie Parker was still beautiful, but appeared to have aged a bit. Asia assumed she was in her early thirties. Working the kind of cases Adam worked had to be mind numbing.

Coleman continued, "Around 7:09 pm, this figure gets off the elevator."

Asia observed a figure dressed in all black exit the elevator. The mystery person was wearing a black ski cap and a large parka. It was chilly yesterday, but not that kind of cold. As the figure moved towards the office doors, Asia noted the body seemed to be tall.

Asia exclaimed, "Stop. Rewind back."

Coleman paused the video and then rewound back to where the figure stepped off the elevator into the hallway.

"The long legs in straight leg jeans, this is a tall person. The shoes are pretty non-descript, brown, but it could be a man or a woman. What do you think?"

Coleman nodded. "I'm gauging this person's height is above 5'10 based on the long legs. We're going to check with ballistics about the angle of the gunshot. That could help us get a better idea of the height." He zoomed in on the hand. "The shooter is wearing black gloves. It's hard to pinpoint any true body characteristics especially with the big coat. I'm thinking he or she carried the gun inside the coat."

Asia nodded. "I would agree. You said you're talking to Adam's assistant. I'm wondering why the door wasn't locked unless Adam instructed her to keep it open for me."

"That's a possibility. I will definitely ask her. Ms. Parker should be here in the next thirty minutes."

Asia took a deep breath. "Mmm. You know

Adam was a womanizer. His shooting may not have anything to do with a client or a court case."

Coleman raised his eyebrows. "Are you trying to move me in the direction of looking at a woman for this? Isn't it more logical to find out what he wanted to tell you?"

"Of course. It's just that Candie Parker, well, she's been with him for a few years. You should know they were involved romantically. I don't know about recently."

Coleman nodded. "Thanks for the info. I need to know as much about Adam Locklear as possible. I mean the boldness of someone walking into his office. This was premeditated. They knew he was going to be there and waited until he was alone, and they had some knowledge of the cameras to conceal their identity."

Asia swallowed. She swung her eyes back to the figure dressed in the large black parka on the screen. "How did they enter and exit the building?"

Coleman pulled up other angles. "Looks like they came up and left from the garage entrance."

The same way she'd entered only a few minutes later. Asia tried to think of the cars that were there last night. She could only remember Adam's white

Mercedes near the door. "I came through the garage. You didn't catch which car they left in?"

"No, a car didn't leave, but I see when you arrived in your car."

She saw her car on the screen and watched as she climbed out of her own car. "You know I don't like being in parking garages, especially at night. I felt kind of creeped out being there last night. Are you saying this person just walked out?"

Coleman looked at her, "They could have been hiding. We know someone traveled back down the elevator, but after that we don't know where they went."

"You have someone looking at all this footage, right? They can't just slip past. You have to look at every single person. Every floor level."

"I have someone on it. Just remember there are a lot floors. Someone could have slipped that parka off at any time and walked out normally. Or they could have had an accomplice pick them up. We'll find them."

Asia nodded, but her stomach was tightening again.

Did the person know I was coming? Whoever did this, did they know I was going to find Adam's body?

Chapter 7

Thursday, November 17 at 4:57 pm

As she peered at Candie Parker from behind the two-way mirror, Asia noticed her blue eyes were red from crying. The few times she'd seen Candie in person, she was always adorned with long eyelashes and ruby red lipstick. Today, her skin was pale and devoid of any makeup.

Unfortunately, her first time seeing Candie was from her backside. Stunned to see the strawberry blond hair and unclothed backside, Asia had locked eyes with Adam. He looked genuinely shocked that she was there. She didn't give him time to explain, instead she'd twirled around and marched out of the office. She was too mad to cry at that moment, but later she anguished over allowing herself to be sucked in by him.

She ignored his phone calls which usually were pitiful voice mails of apologies *and how she came on to him*. The day Brandon assigned her to prosecute a case with Adam on the defense, she decided to kick his butt in the courtroom.

When she did see Candie, usually she'd saunter into the courtroom with some envelope or package Adam needed. He was known for bringing in last minute evidence or some new revelation to the case. A good defense attorney wanted to make the prosecution look like they hadn't done their homework.

Asia always covered all details no matter how minor. Right now, she was wondering about the timing of Candie's exit. Approximately fifteen minutes later someone entered the building. It's possible the killer could have been watching and waiting for Candie to leave.

Asia thought, "But how could someone be so sure they had the perfect opportunity to get Adam?" She paused her thoughts as Coleman sat down to begin the interrogation. Asia peered to the right and noticed Lamb had entered the interrogation room too. A scowl remained stamped on his face.

Candie nervously looked at Lamb as he pulled

out a chair before turning her attention back to Coleman. It was clear who was the good cop in the room. Lamb sat a distance away from the table with his arms crossed.

Coleman started, "Thank you for coming in. We know this is hard on you. How long have you worked with Mr. Locklear?"

"About five years. He was a good boss. Am I some kind of suspect?"

"No, but we've derived you were the last person to see Mr. Locklear alive. Any information you can share with us would help us get closer to finding a suspect." Coleman paused. "I'm curious about Mr. Locklear's work habits. Did he often stay late?"

She nodded. "He comes in late in the mornings usually around 10:00. I arrive at 9:00 to open the office. He usually stays til 9 or 10 most nights. If it was a really big case, sometimes he'd be there all night."

"So he did have a pattern?"

Candie shook her head. "Not really. His schedule depended on his cases. The easy cases, or what he would call easy, sometimes he left before six o'clock in the evening. That was rare though. If it was a challenging case, those were his words, he would be there a long time."

Coleman nodded. "Last night, we showed you exited the building around 6:54 pm. Was that an unusual time?"

"I didn't have a usual time. I stayed if Adam needed me. Sometimes I would stay late too, but lately..."

Coleman nudged, "Lately?"

"I have been having trouble with my son. My mom usually looks after him. But he's eleven and he gets into things when I'm not around. So I've been trying to get home earlier. My mom is getting older and she's been sick."

"I understand. Last night, did you know what Adam was working on?"

Candie shook her head. "Probably one of the new cases. I'm not sure. He could have also been wrapping up things on the officer shooting case. Officer Lane was the last client of the day."

Coleman frowned and peered down at his notes. "Really? Did he stop by? I didn't see him on the calendar other than for the press conference at twelve o'clock noon. Was he in the office another time after?"

"Actually, Adam went to Officer Lane's home during the press conference. It was around three o'clock in the afternoon, I think, when Officer

Lane stopped by the office. I assume he just came to tie up loose ends since the case was no longer being pursued by the district attorney."

Asia watched Coleman. He scratched notes down on his pad like he was trying to solve a mathematical equation. She stepped closer to the glass, wondering what was going through his mind.

She peered at Lamb, who was also watching his partner. *That man is acting really strange.* Maybe it was time for Lamb to retire. He didn't appear to want to participate in the interrogation, but he was scrutinizing his partner.

Coleman finally spoke, either oblivious or uncaring about his partner's stare. "Did you usually lock the office door after you left for the day?"

Good question. Asia waited for the answer.

Candie's lower lip quivered. "Sometimes I did. He would have after hour visitors so I didn't always."

Coleman leaned forward, "So he would let you know in advance if he had a visitor coming, right?"

"Sometimes. Other times people just dropped by the office. He never said I had to lock the door or not. I opened the office in the morning so depending on if I was in a hurry, I would lock it back."

"Last night, were you aware if he had a late appointment?"

Asia could see tears run down the woman's cheeks.

Candie wiped her eyes with her hands. "He didn't mention anything to me."

"Are you okay, Ms. Parker?"

The woman nodded.

Asia felt herself resisting her own emotions. She may have been the one to find him, but Candie worked closely with Adam for years. She was truly grieving.

Coleman said, "We'll wrap this up soon. I know this was a loss for you. Did you speak to him before you left last night?"

Her voice was low like she was losing it. "I always said good night. Last night, he was bent over his laptop as usual. I tapped on his door, but he barely looked up. I asked him if he needed anything. Sometimes he would ask me to pick up some food from the deli or a burger from Joe's Burger Joint. He loved the Angus burgers."

Candie drifted off into a memory only visible by her. She snapped to, looking at Coleman as if she'd been caught. Her eyes were wide. "His last words to me was he would see me tomorrow. Tomorrow is here..."

Coleman scratched some notes on his notepad. "You sure you don't know what case he could have been concentrating on last night?"

She shook her head. "No. I had the feeling he was processing something. Sometimes when he received a new break in a case, he poured over the evidence or new information to see how everything fit together."

Lamb interrupted from the corner of the room. "What kind of information?"

Candie cringed from Lamb's voice. "I don't know. He didn't always talk to me about what he was thinking. He had to process it first."

Lamb leaned forward. "You said sometimes people dropped by the office. Any of them suspicious?"

Candie's eyes flashed. "I wouldn't know. Adam had a wide range of clients."

"He defended murderers." Lamb snapped.

Candie swallowed. "Innocent until proven guilty."

Asia had to smile. Candie had definitely spent enough time around Adam to know his mantra.

Coleman interjected. "So you said Adam didn't really indicate that anyone was coming last night, but you left without locking the door."

Candie's eyes darted. "I was in a hurry. My mom was agitated and my son hadn't gotten home yet." Her face grew red, "He knew better. I left in a hurry because I thought I had to track my son down."

Coleman held up his hand. "It's fine. I understand. I have a daughter. If she's not home at a certain time, I would be heading out to look for her too. I get it."

He has a daughter. Asia shouldn't have been surprised, not everyone was like her, putting life on hold.

Asia noticed Candie seemed to calm down.

Coleman said, "It would help to know of any after hour visitors."

Candie's mouth seemed to droop. "Brooke Cannon stopped by sometimes. She came by Monday evening before I left."

Asia's ears perked up.

Brooke Cannon. Was she Adam's new girl?

Coleman asked, "For the record, who is Brooke Cannon?"

Lamb answered for Candie. "A fellow colleague.

She likes to defend dirtbags like Locklear did. So what were they meeting about?"

Candie's eyes grew angry. "I don't know. I told you I didn't know what Adam did all the time." She heaved. "She's pretty and they've known each other a long time. I assumed they were you know...together."

Asia stepped back from the mirror. *Together.* That made sense that Adam would hook up with another lawyer, but Brooke was competition. Brooke Cannon had a similar reputation to Adam. She also had high-end wealthy clients thanks to the law firm she'd inherited from her dad. If she remembered correctly, Adam used to work for Cannon Law Firm before branching out into his own private practice. Asia wondered if they were meeting for more than just romantic reasons.

She peered back inside the room. Candie seemed more withdrawn than when she arrived.

Or was this jealousy?

With her eyes directed at the table, Candie asked, "Are we finished yet? I really don't have anything more to tell you. I have to get my kid."

Asia raised her eyebrows. It seemed like the mention of Brooke Cannon's name resulted in a change in Candie. Her eyes were angry, not heartbroken like minutes before. Asia kind of felt sorry for her. It couldn't have been easy for Candie to continue working with a man she'd dated only to see him move on to another woman. Why stay? Adam offered a prestigious position even for a paralegal, but there were plenty of opportunities in Charlotte.

Was Candie pretending to be grief-stricken about her boss?

The more Asia observed the woman, the more questions she had. Though Candie appeared genuinely torn-up about Adam's death, something was off. Asia wondered if either of the detectives had noticed.

Asia stared at Coleman who seemed deep in thought. He looked at Candie for a moment before asking, "You mentioned before you left that Mr. Locklear was intense about his work. Are you sure he was looking at his laptop?"

Candie shook her head. "Yes. He took that laptop everywhere. I wouldn't touch his desk. He placed his paperwork in nice neat piles and whatever he was working on, he liked it to stay exactly as he left it."

Coleman stood. "Thank you for coming in, Ms.

Parker. If you have anything else, please reach out to us."

Candie looked shell-shocked, as if she was surprised the interview was over.

Asia stepped out of the room where she'd observed the interview and watched as Candie walked out in the opposite direction.

Asia walked over to Coleman. "So the interview established Adam had a pattern of working late, but it varied by case. Based on Candie's response, Adam was deep into what he was working on, but not so much, because he did respond to her good night. She was in a hurry, so locking the door wasn't on her mind. Plus, she was aware Adam had a female that liked to visit after hours. That female being a colleague Brooke Cannon. Did you notice her reaction?"

"That pretty much sums up the conversation. And, yes, I noticed her reaction." He smiled. "Adam didn't make it easy on the ladies. Anyway, I will check her alibi with her mom and see if I can talk to her son or any of his friends."

"Good. What was that last question about when you were asking about the laptop?"

Coleman took a deep breath. "It occurred to me

while Ms. Parker was talking that whatever Mr. Locklear was working on was missing."

Asia frowned. She thought back to last night trying to remember Adam's desk. She'd hope to bury the only image that came to mind. "I can't say I noticed much other than Adam."

"I know, and I wouldn't expect you to remember. His desk was clean. The laptop was gone. If he had any papers on his desk, the killer swiped them. There was no phone on him. His killer took the time to gather what they needed."

Asia crossed her arms as if a chill ran over her. "So whatever he was pouring his energy over on the laptop could have been what he wanted to share with me."

Coleman crossed his arms. "I'm pretty sure it was now. Why else would someone take it? There had to be something incriminating that someone desperately didn't want found. Probably precious evidence that's been destroyed by now."

Evidence.

Her next thought sickened Asia.

Coleman looked concerned, "What are you thinking?"

"You said his phone was gone. So someone has a history of his calls. Like a call to the DA's office."

She crossed her arms, but she was feeling chilled by the moment. "You know when I was leaving the hospital last night, I kind of didn't want to leave my family. I mean who can resist being around a newborn? But, I keep thinking. What if I had showed up earlier?"

"You could've been killed too."

Asia held her arms out like she could physically push the thought way. "I was creeped out last night even before I reached Adam's office. I wish I'd seen something so we weren't completely in the dark. Adam was so intent on not talking on the phone. I should've made him tell me."

"I'm sure he thought he was being discreet and that he was safe in his own office. Just don't beat yourself up. You never know, something may come to you later. You know what? I'll get you the video from the garage, maybe something will jog your memory."

Asia shook her head, "Okay, I'll take a look. I was moving so fast to get up to Adam's office. I don't know how much help I can be. What else?"

Coleman looked at the board. "I'm going to start talking to Adam's clients. We have forensics at his home. I spoke to his ex-wife, and she'll be flying in from Florida soon."

"You have your work cut out for you. Keep me posted." Asia walked away feeling drained, but pondering her next move. She needed to know what Adam had to tell her. Now that she knew someone nabbed Adam's laptop and phone, every bone in her body screamed it was why he was murdered.

Chapter 8

Thursday, November 17 at 10:15 p.m.

Asia stared at her living room wall. Thanks to having an artistic younger sister, her house walls were lined with a unique artwork series. Toni had painted a series of African American women drawn in different poses with elaborate big hair and pouty red lips. Gifted to Asia on her thirty-eighth birthday, Toni called it the Diva series. The paintings made Asia laugh out loud with joy when she first saw them. Her baby sister had captured her essence in each woman. Some nights, Asia looked at those fellow divas with pride.

Tonight, she wasn't feeling the camaraderie. A mixture of apprehension had pooled in her stomach. Her mind couldn't turn away from her last memory of Adam. The emptiness of his eyes.

She'd seen crime scenes in photos, but not one up-close.

She knew him.

Asia wanted to remember him in a different way so she tried to draw on images of a time when she enjoyed being around him. That was hard because for so long she had stuffed those memories away.

Her wine glass was empty. Tonight, she'd gulped down two glasses of Moscato. To avoid taking work home, she'd stayed at the office as long as she could. When she left, her intentions were to leave her work there.

As she processed Candie Parker's interview, clearly that wasn't happening. Asia couldn't help but think simply securing the door may have helped Adam. Maybe even saved his life...or not. A bullet could have shattered the glass doors. That would have made it messier for the killer.

Then there was Brooke Cannon coming by two nights ago. Maybe she came by frequently.

Was Adam involved with Brooke? If so, were they close enough that Adam felt secure sharing information with her.

She shouldn't have been surprised. Adam liked to date other lawyers. He often told her he felt like lawyers understood each other. In many ways, Brooke was a good fit for Adam.

Better than her.

Maybe she was too close to this one. The phone shrilled, jostling her out of her muddled thoughts. She moved slower than she intended and squinted at the caller ID. Asia let out a soft sigh.

That maternal radar must be on full alert tonight.

Asia answered the phone, "Why are you still up, Mom? I have my excuses."

"To check on you, of course. I saw the news about Adam, honey. Are you okay?"

"Why wouldn't I be? It wasn't like Adam was the love of my life. I fooled around with him during a moment of temporary insanity."

"Okay, well you're in a mood tonight. Not often do you share your love life with me."

Asia giggled. As fast as the giggle escaped, she felt tears sprang to her eyes. "I've enjoyed a glass of wine. Or two. Maybe I had too much."

"Mmmm. It's probably good to put the bottle away now. Sounds like you're mourning. Adam's not the first man you've lost your mind over, but you seemed to cross paths with him all the time. I would say you'd made your peace with him."

"I kind of had no choice." She added. "We were

on opposite sides and one of us had to win the case. I decided I always had to win."

Her mother laughed. "Well, that's my girl."

"Though, I guess you're right. I accepted Adam for who he was, and we had a quirky friendship. Did you know he was always trying to convince me I would do better coming to his side?"

"Defending criminals? I don't know, Asia. Not to speak bad of the dead, but Adam's clients were not your everyday people. On a lighter note, Jo should be home tomorrow. You should check in with her. It will do you good to be around your niece."

"Mmmm. Have you wondered if I would ever give you a grandchild?"

"I hoped you would find someone you loved and settle down first. You're probably the most driven of my children, and I know you've done important things in your career."

Asia thought about Danye Lester's mother from the press conference.

"Am I reaping what I sow? I pursued my career and not marriage and motherhood. Now I want it and think about it all the time. I feel stuck and alone. I'm mean I'm kind of mourning a man who wasn't even worth my time."

"Asia, I don't know the last time you had a talk with God, but He knows the desires of your heart. You need to trust God for a change. As far as Adam, he was a person, maybe not the most likeable person, but he deserves to be mourned. Though he wasn't relationship material, he was a part of your life. Just be patient. You will have your day. We push ourselves with our own deadlines, but God has His own timing. He won't disappoint. Get some sleep. You need to sleep that wine off. Glad I called."

"I'm glad you called too. Goodnight, Mom."

"I love you."

"I love you too."

Asia placed the phone back on the receiver. She stared at the bottle of wine and the wine glass. Asia and her mom did not always see eye to eye, but that woman was her life. If it wasn't for her family, Asia would've made worse decisions in her life.

She grabbed the bottle of wine and the glass. She returned the bottle to fridge; her mind returned to earlier thoughts.

Candie claimed to be oblivious to a lot even though she worked as Adam's assistant. In some ways that seemed strange. Why would Adam not keep Candie in the loop? She wasn't just some ordinary secretary and from what little Asia knew about her, Candie was a paralegal. She had some intelligence and knew her way around laws.

I like intelligent women. They challenge me. That was the line Adam threw at her years ago.

Asia headed back towards her bedroom, pondering again how much information Adam shared with his new lady love, Brooke Cannon.

She slipped under her covers and drifted into the coolness of the sheets. Her mind was slightly woozy from the wine. She could feel sleep ready to pull her in. As she closed her eyes, she pictured Adam's face. A few times, behind the arrogance and irresistible charm, she had seen sadness. She really didn't know Adam.

Do you ever really know anyone?

Chapter 9

Friday, November 18 at 10:09 a.m.

Despite her slow start this morning, Asia was determined to conquer a priority on her to do list. She gulped the black coffee; the bitter hot liquid traveled down her throat. It was a cold morning for the south. She'd turned the car engine off about two minutes ago and could already see her breath in front of her. She thought one more time about calling Detective Coleman. No. This time she wanted to be able to ask the questions.

Woman to woman.

Asia had more in common with Brooke Cannon than she cared to admit. They both were really good attorneys, though she wasn't sure she liked being included as another one of Adam's conquests alongside Brooke and Candie. Adam pursuing her was a surprise. What was more of a shock was she enjoyed her time with him until he screwed it all up.

She sat her coffee cup in her car's cup holder and stepped out into the almost freezing weather. Asia was glad she grabbed her trench coat to cover her legs. She was a pantsuit person, preferring only to bare her legs for the most formal occasions. Today, she pulled out a navy pantsuit from the closet and paired it with a cream-colored short sleeve sweater and a red silk scarf. Asia was tall, acquiring her height from her dad, and she didn't go a day without wearing three-inch heels. Today was no exception.

Asia strutted across the parking lot towards Brooke Cannon's office, her long ponytail blowing in the wind. Brooke's office was located in the northern, elite part of Charlotte, known for its classy restaurants and boutique shops. In fact, one of her friends, Lenora Freeman, owned a bridal shop only two doors down.

Asia pulled out her phone to check the time. It was a little after 10:00 am, the time Cannon Law Firm opened. She pushed open the door and welcomed the warmth by unbuttoning her trench coat.

Brooke's secretary, an older woman with upswept gray hair, looked up. Her gold-rimmed glasses sat on her nose. The woman had deep wrinkles around her eyes and almost appeared gaunt, yet her blue eyes were clear and sharp. "May I help you?"

"Hello, I'm Asia Reed with the District Attorney's office. I was wondering if Ms. Cannon had an opening this morning."

"So you don't have an appointment?" the woman replied sharply.

Asia glanced down at the name sign on the desk. Francis Bishop. "No, Ms. Bishop, I'm here to talk to her about a mutual friend of ours."

"Well…" The secretary stuttered a response, but was interrupted by the appearance of Brooke from the office door behind her.

They were approximately ten feet away from each other, yet Asia felt like she towered over Brooke Cannon. Brooke was a brunette who wore her hair in a stylish pixie cut. Barely five feet, Brooke's small voice and stature was often undermined in the courtroom. Despite her pretty features, she was the bulldog defense attorney no prosecutor wanted to deal with. She rarely smiled.

Right now, her colleague beamed as she stepped

forward. "Asia? This is really a surprise. I know you can't be here for my services."

Asia glanced at Brooke's secretary before responding. "I'm here to ask you some questions." She paused. "About Adam Locklear."

Brooke's bright smile drooped. "Of course. I'm still in shock, but I've been expecting you."

Really? That surprised Asia. "Okay. Can we talk now?"

"I believe my first appointment isn't until 11:00. Right, Ms. Bishop?" She turned to the older woman who was looking intently at both of them.

The woman nodded. "Yes. You have about forty-five minutes."

"Good. Come on back, Asia."

Asia followed her into the office. Brooke's office was conservative, but she had a plush couch over in the corner. Asia commented, "That looks comfortable."

Brooke smiled. "Oh, it is. That couch has been my bed many nights when I couldn't get home. Would you like some coffee?"

"No thanks. I just finished a cup." Asia looked at the wall behind the couch. The wall was filled with picture frames. In the middle was a portrait of a man that looked familiar. She turned and asked, "Is this your dad, Preston Cannon?"

Brooke nodded and walked over with a steaming mug. "Please, sit down. Have you met my dad before?"

Asia sat on a chair opposite Brooke. "No, I've never met your dad, but I've heard stories about him."

Brooke grinned. "I'm sure you have heard stories in the DA's office." She looked up at the portrait like she was not sure she liked it on her wall. "That portrait was painted in his younger days. I was still a little girl." Brooke directed her attention to Asia. "I've thought about taking it down. Even though he officially passed this law firm to me five years ago, he still worked in the office across from me years afterward. Thankfully, he plays golf most days now."

"I bet you're relieved. I was sorry to see my dad retire from force. It was good to have him on the same team. Do you have any siblings?"

Brooke's smile drooped slightly. "Yes. I have an older brother."

"No interest in law, huh?"

Brooke took a long swig of coffee.

Asia observed her hands. She could've been

mistaken, but she sensed a tremor in Brooke's hand.

She finally answered, "My brother, or I should say half-brother, didn't get along with my dad. I think he's still upset that my dad left his mom for my mother." She added. "But, we've always gotten along. He's a great guy, just misunderstood."

Asia shook her head, reminded of a recent conversation with her mother about her relationship with her own half-brother. "Well, you're doing a fabulous job running the practice. I'm sure your dad and your brother are proud."

"Ms. Bishop was his secretary, but she decided to stay on with me. She says she's never going to retire. Sometimes I think she's dad's spy. He seems to know what I'm working on before I tell him."

"Wow. You know Adam always commented I didn't know what I was missing by not being in private practice."

"It's very challenging work, but of course being in the public sector is admirable work." Brooke looked at her, "You've been assistant district attorney for some time. Surprised you didn't decide to give your boss a run for his money this past election. You're probably the kind of district attorney Charlotte needs."

Asia shook her head. "I have no interest in politics."

Brooke smiled, "Not surprised. You're good at what you do."

"That reminds me. What did you mean by you were expecting me?"

Brook sat her mug down and clasped her hands together. "Adam had a lot of respect for you."

Asia frowned. *That didn't really answer the question.* "Are you aware I'm the one who found Adam?"

Brooke's skin paled. She placed her hands on her chest. "Oh my goodness. You saw him... like that? I can't imagine."

"It's still a pretty painful image. He'd called me earlier and asked me to come over."

"I know you two were involved at one time."

Asia held up her hands. "That was ancient history. Not sure how I fell for him at that time in my life, but this was business. He had some information for me."

Brooke frowned, "Oh."

"Problem is, I don't know if I will ever know what he had to tell me."

"That's awful, Asia, but why are you coming to me?"

"You kind of just told me you were expecting me. Candie Parker mentioned you and Adam were close. I wondered if Adam confided in you about anything recently."

Brooke blinked. "No. We tried not to talk about work."

Asia narrowed her eyes. *Now why don't I believe that?* "I see. You were together? A couple. I mean you met him after hours sometimes at his office."

Brooke squirmed in her chair. "Wow. This is awkward. There was nothing serious between us. We were old friends. His office was on the way home for me. I'd stop by to ask him if he wanted a drink. He was fun to be around. You may remember that."

Asia fought an urge to squirm. She'd made the decision to have this conversation. Comparing notes with another woman about a man was not what she had in mind. Asia smiled. "He was a lot of fun."

"You said Candie told you I'd been by Adam's office?"

"She mentioned Adam's work habits, how he stayed late. Sometimes you dropped by. When was the last time you saw him in person?"

"I'm not sure why I was on Candie's mind. It's been weeks since I saw Adam."

That's odd! Candie had mentioned seeing Brooke on Monday. Asia decided to tuck that piece of information away for now. "Well, the times you dropped by, do you remember if the door was locked when you arrived?"

Brooke sat back in her seat and crossed her arms. "I see what you're trying to do. You want to know if somehow the door was left open for the killer. You're not looking at Candie as a suspect, are you? I will have to say I didn't talk to Candie much. I got the impression she didn't like me. Adam told me they were involved once. I suspected she was jealous."

Asia arched her eyebrow. "How jealous?"

Brooke folded her arms. "Not jealous enough to harm Adam. He helped her. Gave her a really good job."

Asia commented, "I don't even know how Adam met her."

Brooke leaned forward. "She was an escort girl."

"What?" Asia stared at Brooke like she was telling a joke. "Really?"

"Yes, she really did study to be a paralegal. It was her escort money that paid for her education."

"I find it strange that Adam would reach out to an escort girl."

"You mean because he could have any woman he wanted."

"Well, yeah."

"I knew Adam a long time. He was insecure in some ways. Especially back then."

Asia tilted her head. *Back then.* She commented, "There was nothing insecure about Adam Locklear."

"Oh, he was really good at letting people see that flawless persona, believe me. I knew him when he was a dorky looking law student working under my father."

Asia had a hard time thinking of the sophisticated man she knew as being dorky. She started to think. "You know, I really didn't know much about his background other than he went through a divorce. His wife took the two kids and moved to Florida."

Brooke pointed her finger. "He'd been so caught up in his career, he really wasn't around for his wife or family. He took the divorce harder than he'd like to admit to anyone. Family was really important to him."

Asia nodded. "Didn't he lose his parents while in law school? Automobile accident, I think."

For the first time since they'd been in her office, Brooke teared up. She touched her fingers to her eyes and sniffed. "Yes. I remember when it happened. I hated to see him in such pain. Adam has always been such a good friend. Very loyal."

Asia frowned. *Loyal.* That wasn't a term she would use for Adam. Although, she did recall Adam commenting once about how blessed she was to have siblings. At the time, she was surprised to hear Adam use the term "blessed." He tended to describe himself as a lucky fellow.

You're my regret. Those were Adam's words to her during that final phone call. Were those words what spurred her to go see him instead of insisting he share his information on the phone?

Asia cleared her throat. "Seems like you did know an Adam I never met."

Brooke cocked her head. "He admired you."

Discomfort snuck back into her stomach as Asia eyed Brooke, "You said that before. How do you know this?"

Brooke wiped her eyes. "You came up in some of our conversations."

Asia raised her eyebrow "I just happened to come up?"

Brooke laughed softly. "Usually after a case you won. He was quite taken by you. Well, he was maddened by you would be a better word. He didn't like to lose."

"Sometimes Adam had clients that were guilty, plain and simple. You can't argue with solid evidence."

"You're right." Brooke bit her lip. "Look, I'm sorry I haven't been much help to you." Brooke hesitated, "I will say this about Adam. He was very conscientious. If he had something for you, he left it in a safe place for you to find."

Asia frowned. "You do know that you're also saying Adam knew something was going to happen to him. Are you sure he didn't confide in you? Was there anything different about him lately?"

Brooke's eyes darted to the clock on the wall. "It's been a few weeks, like I said. Although, we talked on the phone a few times. He seemed distracted, but that wasn't unusual for him."

Asia asked, "Were there any clients that seemed to get under his skin in particular?"

"I told you, we didn't talk about work." Brooke rubbed her shoulders like she'd caught a chill, "At least rarely. One night we did discuss the importance of having protective measures in place. Adam had a unique set of clients. The kind that needed a special lawyer. Some of them were very sick individuals, but some of them had a lot of wealth and power. He was paid well to keep secrets and people out of prison."

"You think he kept some kind of safe or safe deposit box?"

Brooke stood, "I don't know. My dad taught me to always tread carefully when you keep other people's secrets." She held her hand out, "I'm sorry. My client will be arriving soon."

Asia stood and shook Brooke's hand. "Thank you for your time."

"Do you know when they will have services for Adam?"

Asia shook her head. "Well, you know they can't release the body during the investigation. A memorial service would be great, but I don't know who would do that. Maybe his ex-wife. I'm sure he had some friends here in Charlotte who'd like to attend."

"Not a lot of friends. Adam led a lonely life. Sad to say, but his work was his life."

That struck a chord in Asia. "Maybe that's why I related to him so well."

"This life we lead as lawyers. It's not glamorous at all."

Asia said, "No, it's not. Thank you again for you time."

As Asia exited Brooke's office she looked up to see a man in the waiting room. She guessed this was Brooke's eleven o'clock appointment. The man turned to her. His eyes were sharp blue behind the thick framed glasses. For a moment, Asia thought he looked familiar. As she passed by, she caught a whiff of his cologne. It was very strong, spicy. She felt sorry for Brooke for having to have that smell in her office.

Behind her, she heard Brooke approach. Asia turned to see the man stand. He towered over Brooke. The man and Brooke seemed to be having some type of face-off. Brooke glared up at him, "What are you doing here?"

So, he wasn't the next appointment. Asia peered back at Ms. Bishop whose face appeared equally surprised.

Brooke noticed Asia was still there and grabbed the man by the elbow leading him back towards her office. Asia frowned, but then realized Ms. Bishop was approaching her. The older woman asked, "Did you need anything else, Ms. Reed?"

"No, thanks. I'm on my way out." She slipped out the door without looking back. Private practice was definitely not something on her radar. She preferred being a prosecutor, making sure the right people were put away.

When she reached her car, she sat for a moment trying digest what Brooke had shared. Or rather what the woman had selected to not mention. Asia knew there was more purposely left unsaid.

Like why did Brooke conveniently forget she'd stopped by Adam's office on Monday? Or was Candie mistaken?

Brooke brought up her long history with Adam. Wouldn't Adam have confided in a long-time friend? But they were also competitors, and Brooke claimed they'd never discussed work. Asia found that hard to believe because during her many conversations with Adam in the past, he didn't mind talking about his cases. His work was clearly his life.

She pulled out her phone. As she waited, she knew it was time to return to the place she'd been trying to block out of her mind. "Detective Coleman, it's Asia Reed. Would you mind meeting me at Adam Locklear's office building in about an hour?"

Chapter 10

Friday, November 18 at 1:54 p.m.

Coleman didn't look too happy with her as they entered Adam's office building. "Why didn't you let me know you were going to talk to Ms. Cannon? I know I'm new at this, but how this works is I gather evidence and find the suspect. I mean we're a team, right?"

Asia was a little taken aback. "I had a personal conversation with a colleague. If you feel like you need to talk to Brooke Cannon then by all means do that. I would say her conveniently forgetting her recent visit to Adam deserves your questioning. Yes, I'm looking for you to bring me a suspect with some solid evidence. I also need to know why Adam was shot dead right before I went to see him."

She smashed the number on the elevator panel. "Speaking of a team, where is *your* partner?"

Coleman sighed, "I don't know. Something is going on with him. The sergeant seems to be in the know, but she's not saying anything to me." He shrugged. "It's either a case of ready for the pension or I don't really like this here boy as my partner."

Asia glanced at him. "Maybe both. If it makes you feel any better, I don't think he's gotten along with any of his partners. I really didn't mean any harm by not inviting you to my conversation with Brooke. She's a skilled defense attorney. You being in the room would have made her highly suspicious."

The elevator doors glided open and they stepped on. Coleman pressed the button. Asia crossed her arms, unsure if her body was reacting in anger towards Coleman or because she really didn't want to return to the crime scene.

Coleman spoke low as if to calm her. "I'm sorry. I know this can't be easy. Not knowing what's going on."

Asia blew out a breath. "Did you find out anything on Candie Parker?"

He nodded. "Her alibi is solid. Her mom, Helen

Parker, confirmed her story and her son's friend and mom confirmed Candie swung by their house around 7:25 pm to pick up her son. Sounds like she laid into him in front of his friend."

"Glad she found her son. I can't imagine trying to keep up with a preteen boy."

"It's certainly not easy. My daughter is fourteen. Good kid though, but I worry one of these days I'm going to meet a different person in my house."

Asia cracked a smile, thinking, w*ith his good looks, his daughter must be stunning.* She commented, "Hold off on her dating. You being a cop is gonna be a disaster, especially if you were anything like my dad."

Coleman smiled, "Oh, she's got to wait until she's eighteen."

Asia laughed. The elevator stopped. Despite the laughter, she dreaded when the elevator door opened.

Coleman eyed her. "Speaking of suspects, Brooke Cannon shows up every now and then. I would love to know why she forgot to mention Monday evening to you."

Asia stepped into the hallway. "You have the honor of asking her, detective. Although I have to say she doesn't fit though."

Coleman followed her off the elevator, "What do you mean?"

The doors closed behind them. She continued, "Brooke Cannon is petite. She doesn't fit the characteristics of the figure who..." Asia sucked in a breath. "Who stepped off this very elevator in a large parka. Whoever they were, they looked really odd. I'm surprised no one saw anything. This is Charlotte. It doesn't get that cold for that kind of coat this time of year."

Coleman responded, "We're still checking the video footage. The person disappears once they leave."

Asia turned to the opposite office, Advantage Data Systems. "Did you already talk to the people in that office? I mean I'm just curious if they ran into Adam."

"The office looks dark like last time I was here, I will check with the building owner, but I really don't think anyone is occupying those offices." Coleman asked, "Are you sure you're okay with doing this?"

He'd noticed her hesitation.

"Of course." She said, even though the anxiety of walking back into Adam's office made her want to run away screaming.

As they walked closer to the doors of Adam's law firm, Coleman commented. "I do think it's odd with Ms. Parker being his only staff person that he didn't confide in her. It was almost like he didn't completely trust her."

"I agree with you on that. But you know, he could've been protecting her. The information he was keeping could have been dangerous." She grimaced. "The very thing that killed him."

Adan's office door was covered with yellow crime scene tape. Coleman removed the tape so they could enter. Once inside, Coleman said, "The crime scene cleaner has already been in here so you don't have to worry about seeing blood."

Asia nodded. The smell of bleach penetrated the air, but she could still visualize the scene from two days ago. Adam's office door stood open like the night she entered.

Coleman held up his hand. "You should also know most of the prints forensics found were from Locklear and Parker, and I should let you know that Parker had a prior."

Asia arched her eyebrow. "Candie was in the system?"

"She was young, I think twenty. She was

arrested for a DUI. Got off with community service thanks to your boy Locklear."

Asia slowly followed the detective towards Adam's office.

"Really? Funny, Brooke mentioned he met Candie when she was an escort girl." Asia calculated in her head. "She officially started working here about five years ago. Her son is eleven. She'd had to have him pretty young if she is in her thirties. That means she's known Adam a long time. Long before he gave her a job."

Coleman looked at her. "Escort girl, huh? You were right about not ignoring the women in his life."

She stopped in the doorway and watched as Coleman paced the office floor. "I can still see the image of him in that chair. That can't be cleansed from my mind."

Coleman looked back at her. "I can take a look around in here. You don't have to do this."

"No, I'm fine. See if you can find any signs of a safe or locked drawer."

He nodded. Coleman slipped on his latex gloves and placed his hands along the walls. He pulled down a larger framed painting from the side of Adam's desk.

Nothing.

Finally, Coleman walked behind the desk and examined it. Asia watched as Coleman yanked on the desk drawers. All of them opened, one by one. He looked at her. "No secret compartments or locked drawers."

Asia frowned. "Maybe he kept materials in a safe deposit box or his home."

"That's a possibility. We've been to the house, but I'll be heading back this afternoon. What exactly do you think we're looking for? We're still not sure what Adam had to tell you. Would it have been something that was tangible or just information? Maybe he recorded something."

She sighed, "It could have been anything. Whoever did this took everything they needed since they have his laptop and phone. All of that could be destroyed now."

"Unless it's been backed up on a server. Surely Ms. Parker would know how their digital data was stored. He had to trust her enough to keep his client files confidential."

Asia placed her feet fully inside the office. When she found Adam, she knew not to touch him or the crime scene. She turned to her right. "What's in the closet?"

Coleman opened the door. It was the size of a walk-in closet. "Looks like a lot of filing cabinets. We can assign someone to look through the files, but that could be a needle in a haystack. This has to be something recent. The person moved to eliminate Adam with some speed."

Asia walked towards the desk and looked down at the phone. "Perhaps I'm being paranoid, but did you sweep the office for bugs?"

Coleman raised his eyebrow. "No. Wow, you got me really worried now. Why would you suggest that?"

"When I think about that phone conversation, I just wonder if someone heard him on the phone with me. He was anxious about not talking on the phone. I don't think Adam was in his office. I mean this is what you describe as a hit, right? The killer was like some hitman on a mission to kill Adam and grab whatever intel he had."

Asia paced, her thoughts coming faster than she could process. "Adam was still with or he should've just left being with Officer Lane and his family after the press conference ended."

"That's right. I haven't reached out to Officer Lane yet. He's on the list."

"We need to know Adam's frame of mind,

whether he was distracted by a case or something else. Was there someone following him? Someone had to be tracking his movements, finding a pattern. We need any clues we can get."

She stood still. The room felt like the walls were closing in. Asia whirled and stepped out of Adam's office into Candie's office area. She looked over to see a silver picture frame sparkling. A young boy with sharp blue eyes looked back at her. Must be Candie's son.

Behind her Coleman asked, "Are you alright?"

She turned slightly and answered over her shoulder. "Sorry, I'm was getting a bit nauseous. I would like to know more about Candie's history with Adam. Seems a lot further back than I thought. Same with Brooke Cannon too, she knew Adam in law school."

"Do you really think we need to dig into Adam's past?"

Asia turned to face him. "I know you're new to this and it seems like a lot, but we can't afford to ignore anything. It's curious to me that these two women who were closer to him than most people seem to be holding something back."

Coleman scratched notes onto his pad. "I see why you're best."

"You said something about going to Adam's house this afternoon. I'd liked to tag along."

"Are you sure? I mean you have to have a heavy case load."

"I can handle my other cases, Detective Coleman."

"Well, you should know that Mrs. Locklear, Adam's ex-wife is at the house. She's here to take care of his affairs."

"Good. She's probably the best person to talk to about Adam's character. Lead the way. I will follow you in my car."

As they walked out of the office towards the elevator, Asia couldn't help but think she was meeting yet one more woman romantically connected to Adam. While she'd been involved with Adam after his divorce, this conversation could be the most difficult. This was the one woman Adam truly loved.

Chapter 11

Friday, November 18 at 4:04 p.m.

Asia had been to Adam's house once. He lived
in a gated community where the houses were large
with substantial property allowing for privacy. On
this trip, she was more than happy to be alongside
Detective Coleman. She tended not to do
interviews until someone was arrested and charged
with a crime. In the past few days, she'd entered
her sister Jo's role. As she climbed out of her car
to follow Detective Coleman, she heard her phone
beep. She'd checked in briefly with her assistant at
lunch. It was her calling again.

"Yes, Christine, what is it? I'll probably not be
back in the office until Monday. Can this wait?"

"No, ma'am. It's the boss, boss. Hold on."

Asia stopped in her tracks. Coleman looked over

his shoulder at her with a quizzical stare. She held up her hand to indicate he should wait for her.

"Asia, are you okay? You haven't been in today."

"I'm on a case, Brandon. Something wrong?"

"Which case, Asia?"

She frowned, "Adam Locklear, sir."

"Police have a suspect?"

"No. We're working on that now. You did say whatever is found could possibly affect the District Attorney's office. Seemed like a priority from you yesterday. Was I wrong?"

"I'm just wondering if maybe you're too close to this one, Asia."

"I'm fine. We're about to talk to Adam's ex-wife. I will keep you in the loop."

"Be careful, Asia."

"I will." She clicked off the phone. Brandon was right to be concerned, but she wanted to climb out of the dark place that she'd been pulled into since finding Adam's body two nights ago.

"Everything okay," Coleman asked as they walked towards the front door together.

"Just the boss checking in. He's probably having second thoughts about me roaming around on this case."

Coleman said, "I can imagine." He rang the

doorbell and they waited. A minute later the door was opened by a woman.

Asia had seen pictures of Dana Locklear, but this was the first time she'd seen her in person. Tanned, with chestnut brown hair and blond highlights, Dana was dressed in a large shirt and leggings. Asia suspected the shirt belonged to Adam. "May I help you?" the woman asked. Her green eyes were red.

At least the women in Adam's life were grieving for him. He couldn't have been all that bad.

Coleman held out his badge. "I'm Detective Coleman and this is ADA Asia Reed."

Dana looked at them both and then stepped back so they could come inside. "There's a bit of a mess. I'm trying to figure out what to do with Adam's stuff."

Remembering what Brooke asked earlier, Asia inquired, "Will there be a memorial service?"

Dana nodded, "I'm working on it. May not be until next week. The kids are devastated. My parents are looking out for them."

Asia asked, "Your parents are still here in Charlotte?"

"Yes, I thought I would get them to move to Florida before we did, but they like it here."

Coleman responded, "Ma'am, we're sorry for your loss. Can we ask you a few questions about Mr. Locklear?"

She shrugged. "Come into the living room." They followed her through the foyer. The living room looked the same way Asia remembered it years ago. Adam was into sculptures. There were several pieces in various corners.

"Please sit down. I'm not sure how much I can help. I didn't know much about Adam's cases when we were married and the past few years I only called him if the kids needed something."

Coleman asked, "When was the last time you spoke to him?"

"Last week. Dallas, our oldest is looking at colleges. He's real smart like his dad. Thinking about going into law. I'd asked him to call Dallas to discuss the options since Adam was paying the tuition."

Asia touched a nearby sculpture. She asked, "He stayed in the kids' lives?"

"Not much more than when they were here in Charlotte. He was a good provider. When they needed things, he made sure they had what they needed or rather what they wanted."

Asia asked, "How was he on the phone? Could you tell if anything was bothering him?"

Dana nodded, "I could tell he wasn't sleeping."

"You could tell that on the phone?" Coleman questioned.

"I've known the man for twenty years." Dana shuddered, her voice grew hoarse. "I watched him struggle as an unknown lawyer to become this mega-star of lawyers. He was cool and suave in the courtroom, but he didn't handle his personal life so well."

Asia nodded, "Someone I talked to recently mentioned he was insecure."

Dana scoffed, "He was. He grew up sheltered. His parents were religious. When I met him in college he was soft-spoken, kind, and attentive. Over the years, the more his practice grew, the more his personality changed."

Asia couldn't help but think once again she really didn't know Adam. Maybe those sneak peeks into his former personality was what she saw in him.

Coleman asked, "So when you said you could tell he wasn't sleeping, what was he like? Did he not sleep when something was bothering him?"

"Yes, when were married, he would wake up

from really bad dreams. Some nights he would not sleep. He'd slid further and further into a case. I think he was more comfortable with working a case than dealing with life. He'd drink when he felt haunted. The night he called, his voice was slurred and he kept going on and on about regrets."

"Regrets?" Asia repeated. Adam had mentioned that word to her.

"I don't know what he was talking about. It could have been he regretted taking a case maybe. I couldn't tell. I just know I wanted him to talk to his son and he wasn't there."

"When did you and Adam meet?" Asia asked.

"In college. We both graduated and he went on to law school. We had Dallas back then and we struggled. He was idealistic wanting to fight for the people receiving great injustice. I didn't get into his work, but I noticed he was taking clients who really didn't deserve to receive justice."

Detective Coleman said, "Everyone has a right to a fair trial."

Dana smiled, "I'm aware, but some people are just evil. Adam knew that, and he took them on anyway. I think he thought he was building a life for us. This house."

Asia nodded. "Any of these clients, in particular, affected Adam?"

Dana shook her head. "I wouldn't know. I just know he changed over the years."

Asia continued. "Did you know Brooke Cannon? I think she went to school with Adam."

Dana's eyes looked angry. "Yes, I know Brooke. She thought Adam should have married her."

Asia looked at Coleman.

His eyebrows shot up and appeared so comical that Asia had to turn from him. She wasn't surprised. "So they were close in law school? She said they'd been friends a long time."

"He slept with her while I was carrying our daughter, Justine."

So, Adam wasn't loyal. He was a cheater back then.

Asia swallowed, "I'm sorry. I didn't mean to dredge up bad memories."

Dana waved the apology away. "History. Brooke's dad was like a mentor to Adam. I think he wanted Adam to partner with him, but Adam decided to go solo. I do remember it was always a competition between them."

"I see. Do you know Candie Parker?"

"His assistant? I've talked to her on the phone plenty of times. He's known her since she was really young. She got into some trouble. A friend, I don't know maybe a relative, asked Adam to help her."

"You knew they had a relationship?"

Dana rolled her eyes. "It was that relationship that led me to file for divorce."

"Oh."

Coleman cleared his throat, "Ma'am, forensics has already been here, but I'd liked to check Adam's office again."

"Sure, I can walk you back."

Once inside, Coleman looked around. "Do you know if he kept a safe?"

Dana pointed, "Behind the desk."

Coleman walked over. There was cabinetry built into the wall behind the desk. "You wouldn't know how to get in there?"

"Can I ask why?"

Asia answered, "We believe Adam had something he was keeping that—"

"That someone killed him for." Dana shook her head. "I'm not surprised. Adam had visitors and late-night calls that were not always other women."

Coleman nudged. "You sure you don't know anyone in particular?"

Dana shook her head, "No, I just know I heard

more than I wanted to sometimes when I walked into a room. Conversations usually ended with Adam saying, 'I will take care of it.' I always wondered what he meant by that, especially when he wasn't taking care of his family. He loved us, I know that."

Dana walked over to the safe and pressed a variation of six numbers and the safe clicked. She stepped back as if the contents would spill out.

Asia watched as Coleman pulled on his latex gloves. He reached into the safe and pulled out two items, a stack of dollar bills and a notebook. According to Asia's calculation, the stack had to be at least a few thousand dollars. While the money was of interest, her eyes focused on the other item. "What's in the notebook?"

Isaac flipped the notebook open.

Asia leaned in and observed the curvy handwriting. "This is definitely not Locklear's handwriting. It's too feminine." She glanced back at Adam's ex-wife. "Is this your notebook, Dana?"

Dana shook her head. "No. I can see the money. Adam liked to have cash available. But, I'm not sure why he would he keep that in the safe."

Coleman pulled an evidence bag out of his jacket pocket. "We will find out. There's something in this notebook Adam wanted to keep secure."

As they walked out, Asia glanced into a room noticing boxes were stacked up. "It was good to meet you Dana. I'm sorry it was under these circumstances. I know Adam loved you and your children. I think he was kind of lost without you."

Dana twisted the collar of her shirt. "I doubt he was that lost. He was lost after his parents' accident though. He started becoming a different person then, but there was still some good in him."

"You said Adam's parents were religious?"

"Adam's dad was a minister. He married us. His mom stayed at home and homeschooled him. He grew up sheltered. They were killed by a drunk driver. That's why I was troubled when I saw him start to drink."

Asia nodded, "When was the accident?"

"He was still in law school, and we'd just had Dallas. His parents were able to see their grandson, but never met their granddaughter."

"Was he already working with Preston Cannon by this time too?"

"Yes, he was a clerk for Preston Cannon."

Asia held out her hand, "Thanks for talking to us. I'd like to attend the service. Adam and I fought on opposite sides of the courtroom, but I saw the good in him on occasion."

"I'm glad he showed you that side. I felt like it disappeared, like the man I married was gone."

Asia followed Coleman out, pondering the Adam she'd only seen glimpses of on rare occasions. The side of Adam who reached out to her hours before his death.

"I'm going to dig into these finds. As soon as I see something, I will let you know."

"Thanks, Coleman. We make a good team."

Coleman commented, "Do you mind me asking why you asked a lot of questions about Adam's past? Is his past really relevant?"

"I know it may seem like I'm all over the place. I think I'm just trying to get to know him. Sometimes you have to get to know people, what they're thinking, how they'd react, and what their triggers are."

"You're trying to get into his head on that final day?"

"I'm looking to place myself in Adam's shoes and figure out what I would have done with important information. What I have learned today was not totally new. Adam protected his clients, some who had secrets or had done terrible things.

Whatever it was, Adam's conscience, maybe for the first time in a long time, was bothered."

Detective Coleman nodded, "Something scared him. That thing about the wrong man."

"Yes. We have to figure out this wrong man angle."

"Well, I hope you take some time to rest and enjoy family this weekend. One thing I have learned is nothing just falls into your lap during an investigation."

Asia cocked her eyebrow. "Sounds like you're ready for the weekend, Detective."

He smiled. "My daughter is playing tomorrow. She's on the varsity girls' basketball team at Providence. After this week, I'm looking forward to finally catching a home game. I need a breather."

Varsity. His daughter must be really good. "Providence, that's a private school?"

"Yes. One of the reasons why I'm glad to finally move up to detective. My daughter is intelligent and I like being able to invest in her education early."

Asia liked Coleman even more. "You enjoy your weekend, Detective. Good luck to your daughter and her team."

"Thank you. Same to you, Ms. Reed."

She watched as he walked towards his car. Before heading to her car, she looked back at Adam's house. It was a beautiful home and Adam had a family he'd left behind. Asia didn't let much get to her. What struck her most as she opened her car door was how sorrowful Adam's ex-wife seemed to see how much he'd changed.

Funny, it all started under the influence of his mentor Preston Cannon. She needed to take some time for the weekend, but Asia knew digging into Adam's past was the right way to go. She felt it in her gut.

Chapter 12

Saturday, November 19 at 11:15 a.m.

Asia smiled at her brother-in-law when he opened the door. "You doing alright, bro? Looks like you could use some sleep."

Bryan Powell rolled his eyes. "Our daughter is a sweetie-pie, but she does not sleep through the night like BJ. Come on in."

She stepped inside. Asia had to admit she had her doubts about Bryan. She was amazed at how Jo and Bryan turned their marriage around. Then again, she shouldn't have. Their parents' almost forty-year marriage had survived an affair that resulted in her half-brother.

Asia walked past the kitchen and saw BJ munching on a bowl of cereal. "Are you being a good big brother?"

BJ grinned. "Hey, Aunt Asia. I'm a really good brother. Alisa isn't being very nice though."

She laughed, "Why is that?"

BJ held his hands up. "She won't let anyone sleep."

Bryan raised his eyebrow. "Umm, buddy, I think you slept way better than Mommy and me."

"True, I did. But you and Mommy are not looking too good."

Bryan laughed. "You might want to keep that to yourself. Don't let Mommy hear that one."

Asia grinned. "He's being honest. Although I have to agree with your dad. You gotta take it a bit slow with some of your comments."

She walked towards the back of the house where the nursery was located. Jo was dressing Alisa in a pink onesie with yellow dots.

Asia clasped her hands together, "That's the outfit I bought her. She looks like a doll."

Jo grinned. "I told her I sensed her auntie Asia would be over today so we needed to dress her up. You want to hold her?"

"Sure. I would love to." Asia held out her arms. Her heart melted as she inhaled the baby's sweetness.

"How are you doing?" Jo asked.

"Me? You're the one who just delivered a seven-pound diva."

"And you walked in on a... crime scene. Somebody finally got to Locklear, huh?"

Asia kissed her niece on the forehead. "Yeah. I shed a few tears for that joker. Nobody, not even Adam, deserved to go out like that."

"You two had a special kind of relationship."

"I wouldn't call it special. He left an impact though. He's not a person you forget." Asia handed Alisa back to Jo. "I'm learning a lot about him after his death."

Her sister looked at her. "Like what? You have that funny look on your face."

"What funny look?"

"The one where something's really bothering you, but you pretend like you're all good."

Asia rolled her eyes. Then she picked up one of the stuff animals from the nursery shelf. She held it in her arms. "You know how you told me when you had this gut feeling about a case?"

"Yeah, I'm sure you experienced it a few times. You know what's needed for a case to make it to trial. You know how the other side is going to run the defense."

"No, that's different. That comes from knowing

and interpreting the law. This is something else, more your area." Asia took a deep breath. "I found Adam that night. I was there because he had something to tell me. I have no idea what he wanted to share, but my gut says it's why he was killed."

Jo switched her daughter to her other arm. She responded low, "What? Oh my goodness, Asia. Mom didn't tell me that."

"Because I didn't tell her. Don't you go telling the rest of the family either. I just needed to get this off my chest. Sorry, you're it!"

Jo sat down in the rocking chair. "Dang, girl. That's a pretty heavy load to be walking around with on your mind. Do you have any leads?"

She shook her head. "I looked over the footage with Detective Coleman. There was a figure who walked out the elevator. They're wearing a big coat like what you need to carry a gun. They knew the building and how to avoid the cameras. We've been talking to people and I know people know more than what they're actually saying."

Jo raised her eyebrow. "Did you say Detective Coleman? That name sounds familiar."

Asia waved her arm. "He's new. His partner is Detective Lamb."

"Ugh, poor guy. Lamb is the worst. He needs to just retire and enjoy his pension."

"Yeah, well you know Lamb didn't care about Locklear. He's not even showing his face for this investigation."

Jo shook her head. "That's a shame. He must still have a chip on his shoulder. It was Lamb's fault that guy got off. That was about four years ago now, right? He knew better than to not preserve the crime scene. And the knife suddenly showing up. He practically gave Adam something to use against him on the stand."

"Yeah, well he had the nerve to accuse me of killing Adam."

"What? Has he totally lost his mind? You were probably one Adam's handful of friends."

Asia wrinkled her nose. "Friend is a strong word. Plus, he had another female to keep him company these days. Brooke Cannon."

Jo arched her eyebrow, "You sound jealous."

Asia jabbed a finger in the air, "Okay, now you're tripping from a lack of sleep." She turned and paced the nursery. "You may want to brace yourself for this one."

Jo responded, "Uh oh."

"I met Adam's ex-wife yesterday. I can't seem to

avoid the awkwardness of this situation if I tried. I knew Adam had been married, but I'd never met his kids, and really didn't know what his life was like. But, it seems he was an average guy in another life."

"Average? The debonair Adam Locklear was special and I don't mean in a good way."

"I know. According to his wife he'd changed over the years. He became this really unlikeable person especially after working under Preston Cannon." Asia crossed her arms. "You know, as many times as Adam got under my skin, I occasionally saw that good side. Did you know his dad was a minister?"

Jo stretched her eyes, "Wow! They say you never really know a person."

"Yeah, you're right about that. The crazy thing is I think Adam was choosing to do the right thing, maybe for the first time in a long time."

Alisa stirred a bit. Jo had stopped rocking. She pushed her feet to move the chair again. "I'm sorry. I know this must be hard on you. It's been what, three days? Something will come up soon. Sounds like you're really grasping at a lot of information though."

Asia peered over at Alisa. "She's so sweet and

innocent. Born into a crazy world. I feel obsessed and not in a good way with Adam's life."

Jo looked at her. "You want answers. Adam may find some way to get you that information."

"I don't need him to reach out from the grave."

"Not creepy like that. I'm just saying don't lose faith." Jo yawned. "Let's let her sleep. Unfortunately, this isn't going to help us all later when she's wide awake tonight. I need some coffee."

"Possibly more like a nap."

"I have plenty of time for a nap." Asia followed her to the kitchen. They passed Bryan and BJ who were playing an Xbox game.

Asia commented, "The boys are having fun."

"Yeah, as long as they don't get too loud." Jo grabbed mugs from the cabinet. She poured coffee in both mugs and passed one to Asia. They both walked over to the kitchen table that faced the patio. Asia spent so much time indoors, this was the first time she'd noticed autumn was moving in. During the spring and summer, the patio was plush with green. Now, leaves were piling up and blowing across the concrete area.

Asia hated to break the mood, but she had to

ask, "Will you ever return to homicide? You were so good."

Jo shrugged. "One day I'll go back. It's in our blood. The Reeds like to get the bad guys. I kind of miss it. I just don't need all the craziness right now."

"I get it. For the first time in a long time, I don't really like being an ADA."

Jo's smile disappeared. "I know it's rough putting bad guys away, but I've never heard you talk like this before. Is Adam's death bringing all this on?"

"It's more than Adam. It really started with the Danye Lester case. I wanted to bring that family some justice."

Jo sighed, "I have to say as a mom of a little boy who's going to grow up to be profiled, I hoped for once, someone would get punished for taking drastic measures. Officer Lane is not a good cop."

"I heard that a few times, but we know cops are a tight knit bunch. Nobody was going to rat out their colleague because he's not a goody two shoes. It burns me that young man ran, and then he reached for his pocket. It was a classic scenario. He was a good kid. If only Officer Lane could have taken a different action besides reaching for his gun."

They sipped quietly.

Jo broke the silence. "Is Detective's Coleman's first name Isaac?"

"Yeah."

"Is he tall, light-skinned brother?"

Asia nodded. She could picture him vividly in her mind. "Not bad looking at all."

"I just thought of this. He was the officer-on-duty for a few of my cases. In fact, I want to say his former partner was Officer Lane."

Asia almost let the warm mug slip from her hand. She stared at her sister. "Are you sure?"

Jo shrugged. "Ask him. I think they were partners. I remember an Officer Isaac Coleman mentioning to me he wanted to move up and become a detective one day. He was really interested in how we gathered evidence."

"Coleman never mentioned that." Asia thought about how much she'd revealed to him over the past few days about her relationship with Adam.

Jo shrugged, "Maybe he didn't want to be associated since he'd moved on in his career. Plus, Officer Lane has been in the spotlight for a few months now."

"Right?" Asia felt warm all of a sudden.

Jo smiled, "He's a good-looking guy. Is he married?"

Asia smirked. "He wasn't wearing a ring that I saw."

"Mmm, you were looking?"

"I always look, Sis. Now, I plan to do a little digging. I want to know why Coleman never mentioned Officer Lane."

"Why should it matter? You're both working on Locklear's case."

"Everything matters. You just said ask him."

Jo sighed. "I didn't mean ask him right now. Today is Saturday. You're supposed to be enjoying the weekend, but you're here obsessing over a case."

"When have you known me to totally take a weekend off?"

"This time you should. You're too close to this case. I'm surprised Brandon is letting you do this."

Asia sat back, "I'm pretty sure he's going to yank me off eventually. He knows I will find out the information Adam had to share. My boss described me as relentless once. I'm not sure if that was a compliment or not." Asia stood and took her coffee cup to the sink. "I need to go. It was good seeing you guys this morning. Get some sleep."

Jo stood, "Where are you going in a hurry? Please don't be hard on Detective Coleman about the partner thing. The guy I remembered wanted to move on to something new."

"I get it. I'm going to catch a basketball game."

"A basketball game?"

"His daughter is playing a game today down at Providence."

"Are you kidding me? You're really going to interrupt the man during his family time?"

"Not interrupt, just ask a few questions." Like why didn't he mention Officer Lane. In the past few days, Asia had tired of grown folks not telling the whole truth and holding tight to information.

Chapter 13

Saturday, November 19 at 2:15 p.m.

Asia couldn't remember the last time she'd been to a live sporting event. It took some time, but Coleman wasn't hard to spot inside Providence's gym. Dressed down in a t-shirt and jeans, he was definitely more dad today than detective. She almost turned around thinking maybe she should avoid bothering him at his daughter's game. It appeared the game was at the end of the second half, and she was already here.

Why am I here?

It wasn't like her to be impulsive. She tended to think things through, maybe too much. One thing for sure, she was tired of people hiding things the past few days.

Asia looked at the clock, the game was almost

over. She scanned the court and observed a bright-skinned girl with a ponytail puff. She wondered if the girl was Coleman's daughter. Swish. By the looks of the ball hitting the net, she was really good. The time ran down and the crowd on her right side went wild. Asia could no longer see Coleman since most of the crowd were on their feet. She'd headed back towards the parking lot, feeling somewhat foolish. She should've stayed at Jo's a bit longer.

After what seemed like a long time, she finally spotted Coleman. She was right, the girl who threw the last shot was his daughter.

Thinking about her sister's warning, Asia hung back for a moment and watched Coleman interact with his daughter. She thought back to when she was that age and she'd look for her dad in the stands. Justice Reed was a dedicated cop and often left his wife, Vanessa to be the main sideline supporter.

Okay, Asia, you might as well talk to him. She promised herself to only be a few minutes. If anything, she wanted Coleman's reaction and then she was gone.

"Coleman, how are you? Is this your daughter?"

Coleman whirled around. He seemed surprised

to see her at first, but then a smile spread across his face. "Ms. Reed, I didn't know you were going to attend the game."

"Actually, I'm here to ask you a few questions."

Coleman's smile disappeared. "Today?"

She added, "It will only take a few minutes, but introduce me to this star player first."

Coleman's daughter stared at her. "Thanks. Are you a lawyer? I think I saw you on TV."

Asia nodded. "I am a lawyer. Asia Reed." She held out her hand.

Coleman's daughter shook her hand, "Imani Coleman. I want to be a lawyer when I grow up."

Coleman looked at his daughter. "I didn't know that."

Imani looked at her dad like he didn't have a clue. "What, you thought I wanted to be a basketball player?"

Asia laughed, "Smart girl. She's making good plans at a young age. Maybe one day I can show you what I do."

"That would be awesome. Hey, Dad, I want to go with Tessa and her mom."

Coleman frowned, "I thought we were headed to have a victory meal."

"Well, I'm spending the night with Tessa so I

may as well go with them now. That will save you the trouble of having to drop me off later."

Asia noticed a tall, slim girl with exquisite dark skin a few feet away. She also wore her hair in a ponytail puff. They were beautiful girls. Asia eyed Coleman to see his reaction.

He hesitated, "I guess you have a point. I expect you to be in church tomorrow. We can have brunch after service. That sound like a plan?"

"You're the best, Dad." Imani hugged her dad and he hugged her back.

Coleman watched his daughter run off with her friend towards a waiting van. Asia assumed the woman waving back was the mom. Coleman waved before turning around to face her. He appeared sorrowful, like he'd lost something precious.

She cleared her throat, "I'm sorry if I messed up your plans. I really just had a few questions."

"It's fine. I'm pretty sure my daughter wanted to hang out with her friends all this time. She's not a little girl anymore and hanging out with Dad isn't cool."

"I don't know, I'm sure she's glad to have you in the stands. I remember being on the court looking for my dad. I would see my mom with my younger siblings, but wondered if my dad would make it."

"I didn't know you played ball, Counselor."

"Yeah, can't say I stay as athletic these days. Funny how my siblings and I took up law enforcement. Looks like your daughter wants to do the same."

"Yeah, I guess I'm not as tuned in as I thought. Now that you're here, shall we grab a bite to eat? Then you can ask me your questions that couldn't seem to wait until Monday."

Asia grimaced. "I'm sorry. How about I follow you?"

Even though it worked out with his daughter going off with a friend, she felt like she'd invaded Coleman's personal time. She followed him a few blocks to Applebee's. Coleman stood waiting for her at the door. She asked, "Was this where you and your daughter were going?"

"Her favorite place." He held the door open for her.

Awkward.

A bubbly teen came up and asked, "Are the two of you dining with us today?"

"Yes." They both spoke at the same time.

They followed the host back to a booth, and

Asia wondered why she just didn't ask her questions and go. Eating lunch together wasn't in the plan. Of course, she'd left Jo's house with no plan other than to find Coleman. She really didn't do well with not thinking things through.

They sat and perused the menus for a while. Asia ordered an iced tea, and Coleman ordered a Coke. When the server walked away with their orders, he asked, "Are your questions about the Locklear case?"

She glanced out the window before addressing his question. "More about your former partner. I was talking to my sister, Jo, this morning. She remembered when you were an officer."

He narrowed his eyes, as if he wasn't sure about her angle. He finally spoke, "Your sister was encouraging. She let me see how detectives processed the scene."

"How come the other day when we talked about going to see Officer Lane, you didn't mention you were partners?"

Coleman placed his hands on the table in front of him as though he was bracing himself. "I don't know. A lot of reasons." He shrugged. "I don't like the guy. He was, in many ways, a worse partner than Lamb. Lamb just ignores me which is fine with me. Lane was a bit of a bully. Not that he got in my way. I didn't take anything from him. He didn't like it, but he had to respect it. I saw the way he treated other guys like he was some demi-god or something."

"None of them would say anything about his character other than he was a good cop. Do you think he was probably over aggressive with pulling the gun on Danye Lester?"

"I wasn't there, Ms. Reed. Events showed Officer Lane pulled the gun in self-defense. Unfortunately, your folks let Lane off the hook if there was something different."

Asia sat back in her seat. *That stung.*

"I'm sorry, I didn't mean to say it like that."

"No, you're right. We looked at the Facebook video. The way Officer Lane approached and how he talked seemed like he was capturing a kid who'd ran himself into a corner. You guys are trained to take people down without having to shoot, but Danye reached for his pocket."

"That's right. The kid ran. He got to a wall that he couldn't scramble across fast enough. And—"

"A cell phone. That's all that was in his pocket."

"Officer Lane isn't the world's greatest cop, but he didn't know. You grew up in this world. Your dad. Your sister. They have to think fast or be killed."

"I know. I've been over all of this more times than I wanted to." She observed the waitress approaching with steaming plates. Coleman had ordered steak with a skewer of shrimp, while she opted for a chicken salad.

They ate in silence for a while before she asked another question. "In what ways did Officer Lane bully? Is there a chance the story wasn't told truthfully?"

Coleman chewed thoughtfully. "I thought you were on the Locklear case now?"

"Locklear was Officer Lane's lawyer. You said in your findings he was the last client Locklear saw."

"Are you trying to connect him to Locklear now? The charges were dropped. They were finished with each other."

"When are you going to ask him about his last visit with Adam? Maybe he noticed something."

Coleman studied her. "You want to get Lane on something?"

She shook her head, "No, that's not what I'm doing here. I want to know what was said. Keep in mind when Locklear called me, he had to still be at Lane's house or maybe he'd just left, but this was right after the press conference." Asia leaned in, "Here is another question for you. How was Officer Lane able to afford Locklear on his salary? Locklear's clientele were normally pretty wealthy people."

Coleman paused.

Asia could see when the light went on his eyes.

He finally responded, "I don't know. Maybe Adam took him on for the challenge. You said he never won a case against you. Suppose he thought he could on this one."

Asia pulled her napkin out of her lap and placed it on the table. "No. Adam wasn't that desperate. He liked to get paid."

The waitress came with the check and handed it to Coleman.

"I can get mine."

Coleman looked at her, "I can afford to take care of the check."

"Touché." She waited as Coleman swiped his credit card on the table register. After he signed the receipt, he looked at her. "Since we seem to be working, you want to talk to Officer Lane?"

"Now?"

"I know where we can find him if you want to lay

your mind to rest. Just know Sundays are off limits for me. After today, I'll see you again on Monday."

She smiled. "I'm not a heathen who works all the time. I just needed to know..."

"I know. What was serious enough for Adam to be killed? Who's to say you're not in some kind of danger? I've been concerned about you."

Asia raised an eyebrow. "Is this why you didn't make me feel bad about tracking you down at your daughter's basketball game?"

Coleman nodded. "I'm new to homicide, but I have no intentions of having you as one of my cases."

Asia followed him outside. She was on her way to her car, when Coleman insisted, "Ride with me. We'll pick up your car later."

She followed him to his Ford Explorer. He held open the door. Once he climbed inside the driver's seat, she questioned, "Are you sure about this? We're off the clock."

"What else am I gonna do? My daughter's at a sleepover."

"Yeah, but your..."

Coleman looked at her, "My daughter's mom. We never married. Her mom's serving time."

Asia had to catch her jaw from dropping open.

That was the last thing she expected to hear. "Serving time for what?"

"Murder. She shot her uncle. Claimed he'd abused her as a child."

"What? Oh my goodness. How do you do it? Imani is really—"

"Well-adjusted. I'm a man of God. I'm not ashamed to pray. When I wanted to get promoted to detective, God answered a prayer that I'd had as a young boy. Let's find out what Lane knows about his former lawyer."

Asia nodded. She was at a loss for words as her admiration for the detective grew.

Chapter 14

Saturday, November 19 at 5:11 p.m.

Her admiration for Coleman dipped as they entered the bar. When she'd said it was okay to meet with Officer Lane, she didn't envision a smoky bar scene. The rank smell was going to be all in her clothes. Maybe it was good he insisted she didn't drive her car over here.

Coleman looked at her, "Lane will most likely be in the back playing darts. It's his thing."

"You sure we should be talking to him while he's throwing sharp objects?"

"Hey, you wanted answers." Coleman moved ahead of her to lead the way.

Once again, she wondered why she didn't stay at Jo's longer today or head home to enjoy the weekend like a normal person.

They walked through a door leading to the game area, and Asia noticed stares from men, mainly law enforcement types as she passed by. Lane was in the back like Coleman had said. She was even more surprised to see Lamb. She peered over at Coleman, who looked equally surprised.

He drew closer. "Well, Ms. Reed. Seems like my current partner and former partner are friends."

Lamb scowled. "What are you two doing here?"

Lane eyed them as they approached. He twirled a dart in his hand. "I heard about your promotion. Congratulations, Coleman. Didn't know you had a thing going with the ADA."

Asia stepped forward. "I'm here about Adam Locklear."

A look flashed across Lane's face that she couldn't read, but it made her focus on him.

"Oh yeah. A shame what happened, he was a good guy."

Coleman commented, "A really good lawyer. Expensive too."

Lane stated, "He respected cops. Knew I was doing my job." He turned and threw the dart at the board. The dart almost landed in the center.

Lamb growled in the corner. "He didn't respect cops."

For once, Asia was grateful to have the curmudgeon speak up. She shifted her eyes to Officer Lane's face. "Lamb's right. Locklear threw him under the bus while he was on the stand. Made a mockery of him."

Lamb guffawed, "You don't have to exaggerate. Your dad, the chief, didn't help either. I'm going to get a refill." He walked away.

Coleman looked after his partner. "You got this?"

She nodded as Coleman went after his partner.

Asia turned her attention to Lane. "Adam was good. No one deserves to go out like that. He had two kids."

Lane nodded "I know. Our kids are the same ages." He grabbed a swig of his beer before continuing. "He was real sure of himself that he would've won if we went to trial. The kid reached for his pocket. I had to make a quick decision."

"I'm not arguing with you. I went through the facts of this case more times than I care to count."

"Then, you should also know there is nothing more in this world I wish I could change. I wish I never saw that kid."

Asia stared at Lane for a moment. The true victims were Danye's family, but as she looked at

Lane's stubbled face and his eyes, she realized probably for the first time that the officer was in pain too. "My family is in law enforcement, Officer Lane. I know it's never easy to take a life or see a life snuffed out."

"That young man haunts me. Not like some ghost, but... my family is destroyed. My kids don't talk to me, my wife barely talks to me. The guys at work are supportive, but even they keep an arm's length. That night... I dream about it over and over."

This wasn't what she expected when she came here. Whenever she saw Lane, he seemed to have more of a smirk on his face. This guy in front of her now looked exactly as he described. Haunted.

"I'm not here about Danye Lester. I do want to know your whereabouts the day your lawyer was killed though. I understand you stopped by his office later in the afternoon after the press conference. Is that correct?"

Lane narrowed his eyes. "Yes, around three-o'clock. Later that night when he was shot, I was home with my family, having an argument with my wife. I'm sure she won't mind confirming. I came here afterwards." Office Lane reached for his beer, but then stopped, "You should know Locklear and his assistant were a bit tense when I arrived."

Asia inquired, "What do you mean?"

"You know how people are all tense after an argument. Like when I argue with my wife and we're both huffing and puffing afterwards. She goes off to her corner and…" He smiled, "I usually come here."

"Did you hear what they were arguing about?"

"No. She definitely wasn't happy, slamming the desk drawers. I felt like I'd came at a bad time."

Asia nodded. "Anything else?"

"What else would there be? You're not hoping I will spill some secrets to you? I mean Locklear is dead, but I don't need to tell you anything we talked about."

"Unless you had something to do with his death."

Lane laughed. "Why would I kill him?" He stepped towards her. "You trying to pin something on me because you couldn't with that kid? Is that what this is about?"

Even though Lane had closed the gap between them, Asia didn't budge.

Coleman came up from behind, "Hey, you should back up."

"Because you're going to defend your girl?"

"She's an ADA."

Lane spat, "I don't care. You shouldn't have brought her here. I've answered your questions. Now leave me alone."

Coleman touched Asia's shoulder. "Let's go."

They walked out together. She didn't speak until they were in the car. "Does it seem like he's hiding something? He purposely mentioned Candie was arguing with Locklear. People argue and she has an alibi. I need you to check his exact whereabouts. He says he came here after arguing with his wife."

Coleman stuck the key in the ignition, but faced her. "Candie didn't say anything about an argument. She could've decided to leave that out purposely."

"I'm curious if there was really an argument, but I'm more curious about your old partner."

Coleman frowned, "What would his motive be for killing his lawyer?"

"I don't know. Maybe Locklear knew something. You did notice that he suddenly got all huffy like I was trying to ask him about what he talked about with his lawyer. I didn't ask him that specifically."

"You don't miss much, do you?"

"I don't know. I feel like I keep missing something. I feel like we have a lot of folks telling half-truths. One of those people hold the key."

"Well, I'm sorry meeting Officer Lane didn't help you getting any answers."

Asia took a deep breath. "It's fine. He was probably right. I'm still steamed about Danye and the fact that I couldn't do anything. But he's haunted. He admitted it." She turned to face Coleman, "Does that mean he's remorseful?"

"It means he's not totally cold-blooded. He didn't just take the man's life to do it. It was self-defense."

They sat in silence. Coleman let out a long exhale. "This trip kind of worked out in a weird way. I finally got to talk to my partner. Though he wasn't exactly sober."

Asia sniffed her shirt sleeve. "Good. Something good came from going in there."

Coleman smiled, then his smile disappeared.

"What's wrong?" Asia asked.

"Looks like I will get a new partner soon. Lamb is retiring. He has stage 4 liver cancer though. Not much of a retirement."

Asia observed Coleman as he turned on the

engine and drove out the parking lot. Asia decided she needed to enjoy what was left of her weekend.

Chapter 15

Monday, November 21 at 10:15 a.m.

Five days ago, she'd found Locklear with a fatal shot to his forehead. Her niece was almost a whole week old. The joy and sadness of that day weighed on Asia for the remainder of the weekend. She really needed more leads this week versus endless questions. Asia clicked the secure URL on her computer so she could view the footage from the garage the night she arrived to find Adam's body.

Lord, you don't hear from me often, but I just need something to resurface that points in the right direction.

That was her prayer as she sat with her family yesterday at Victory Gospel Church. She'd missed a few Sundays prior. Despite running around on Saturday with Coleman, she was ready for some spiritual fuel. She liked that Coleman insisted he and his daughter attend church Sunday. Asia had taken note of Coleman's ability to handle the pressure of the case like a pro despite his newness to investigations. She hated to admit that she'd become quite curious about his life, especially after his admission of his daughter's mother.

He is a single dad, doing it all. What's not to like about that?

Asia stared at the footage for what felt like the tenth time. No other person was visible in the garage when she'd arrived. She'd asked for footage from the time she arrived until she left which was about a three-hour period.

Adam's law firm was in a busy office building. Though it was after hours on a Wednesday night, Asia felt like there should have been more people stirring around the building and garage. The more she looked at the footage, the more she felt like something wasn't right. She just couldn't see it.

Someone knocked on her closed office door interrupting her intense focus. She called out, "Come in."

Her assistant Christine stuck her head in the door. "Hey, Asia, the big boss wants to see you."

"Okay, thanks. Let Brandon know I'm on my way." Asia had promised to keep the DA in the loop, but she'd been avoiding him all morning. It was hard to figure out what to tell him since she still wasn't sure herself. She strode down the hallway towards Brandon's office and knocked on his open door.

Brandon was on the phone, but waved for her to come in. He pointed towards the door, so she closed the door behind her. The door's click seemed too loud to her ears. As she sat down in the chair across from the desk, she heard Brandon say. "Yes, Captain, I will look for Ms. Reed to update me. Thank you."

Oh, that couldn't be good. She straightened her coat jacket so it hung smoothly across her hips.

Brandon smiled, "Asia, how are you doing?"

"You mean what have I found out about Adam Locklear?"

He grimaced, "No, I want to know how you're doing first? Surely you don't think I'm that callous, Asia?"

"Of course not." She fidgeted. "No one can do this job like you, boss. Your passion. Your drive. All admirable."

"I appreciate the flattery, but we both know you can do this job better than me."

Asia tilted her head. "You know I have no interest in politics."

He laughed. "Being a DA is not an easy job. It's very public, but I have no doubts if you run someday, you would easily win the hearts of the people."

She observed him. "You were just re-elected for your second four-year term. Why are you trying to throw me in this ring?"

"Never too early to start planning. I just want you to think about it. Sometimes change is good."

Asia shook her head, flabbergasted by Brandon. "You have over fifty assistant district attorneys. I'm sure one of them will want to step up to the plate if you decide you're ready to move on."

"But you're the best."

"Now I'm flattered. The only thing I want right now is to find out who killed Adam Locklear and what information he had to share with me."

Brandon sat back in the chair across from her desk. "That's what concerns me. It's time we talk about Locklear."

Asia wasn't sure she wanted to know what her boss had to say, but she had a sinking feeling she already knew.

He sighed, looking more exhausted. "I know you

were close to Adam at one time, and I can't imagine what that was like to find him. I wanted to give you some time, but I think you're spending way too much time on the investigation. Why don't we let the detectives do their job? Find a suspect, make an arrest and we will deal with this later. We have plenty of other cases I need you to chair."

"To be honest, I'm surprised you haven't stopped me by now knowing my past history with him."

"I've seen the last week take a toll on you. I need my top ADA back. Plus, you already know, if and when we charge someone, it's probably best someone else on the team serve as the first chair."

Asia nodded. "You're right. It's time for an actual case that has a suspect with solid evidence and witnesses." She grimaced. "Coleman seems to be doing a good job despite being new. He may find something."

Asia thought she wasn't going to hesitate to ask questions either. She felt comfortable with Coleman and knew he would keep her in the loop.

"Good, that's the spirit. Let's talk about where we need to direct your attention to next." He reached for a folder on his desk. "I'd like to see if we could move the Lawrence Warren case forward to a grand jury in a few weeks, definitely before the end of the year."

Asia thought for a moment. "Lawrence Warren, he was one of Adam's clients. He already found a lawyer to take his case?"

Brandon smirked, "Yes, apparently Brooke Cannon was more than ready to help him. Her and Adam were rivals, so I'm not surprised she'd snap up his clientele."

Asia twisted her hands. "Did you know Adam clerked with her dad, Preston Cannon?"

Brandon's face grew pensive, "Yes, I remember when Adam worked under Preston. A lot of lawyers worked under that man. He was good, one of the best defense attorneys around for years. I can tell he groomed his daughter well and you could see where Adam developed his courtroom skills over the years."

"According to Adam's ex-wife, Brooke was interested enough in Adam that she wanted to be Mrs. Locklear."

Brandon raised his eyebrow. "Really? That's interesting. I would keep that under your belt. Brooke's even trickier in the courtroom than Adam."

Asia asked, "I know this is off-topic, but we are

getting ready to deal with Cannon Law Firm. Is Preston officially retired or does he still play a role in the firm?"

"As far as I know, his daughter handles most of the cases. I've seen Preston here and there on the golf course. He's still plenty sharp too. I know he's a board member on quite a few boards here in Charlotte. Very wealthy guy. Why are you asking?"

"I don't know really. I went to talk to Brooke about Adam. She alluded to the fact her dad still keeps up with the firm."

"I'm not surprised. He established Cannon Law Firm almost thirty years ago. Preston was and still is an intimidating guy. In and out of the courtroom. Which is why you need to study this case. Brooke learned from the best." Brandon handed her the folder.

Asia grabbed the folder. "So Lawrence Warren is claiming he didn't shoot his wife, but the evidence says differently?"

"This is premeditated. We need the grand jury to see Warren for what he really is. A cold-blooded murderer. Start preparing. I'd like us ready to do jury selection soon after Thanksgiving."

"I see you really want to get this one moving before the end of the year."

"It's a big case, Asia. One of those ones you can certainly add to your list of wins."

"I'll get on it." Asia rose from the chair.

"Asia?"

"Yes."

"I'm really sorry about Adam, but I think this will be good to get you back in the swing of things. You'll see."

As she left Brandon's office, she knew pushing Adam's death to the back of her mind was necessary. Unfortunately, her unanswered questions weren't going away anytime soon.

Chapter 16

Tuesday, November 22 at 2:15 p.m.

Asia didn't often bring cases home, but last night she did. She needed to make an effort to re-focus her mind away from Adam's death. Only problem was, the more she read through her new case, the more disturbed she'd become. She stared down at her desk, her eyes transfixed on the photo of the slain woman. Something about the way Janice Warren was shot was an eerie reminder of another crime scene in Asia's head.

"Boss, you okay? You need some coffee?"

Asia looked up to see Christine at her door. "Yes, that would be great." She waited until her assistant returned with the cup of coffee.

"Thanks, Christine. This was right on time."

She took a sip of the bitter liquid. "Did you read over these files yet?"

"For Janice Warren? Christine nodded, "Yes, I did. Her husband, Lawrence Warren, claimed he received a text from her. Which we do have evidence of on his phone. When he arrived, he found her shot in her home office. There were no signs of forced entry. No fingerprints other than his and hers in the office."

Asia questioned, "What do you think of his supposed alibi prior to his claimed arrival?"

Christine sat down in the chair across from Asia's desk. "He claims he was working late when he received the text. No witnesses saw him leave work since it was after hours. He could have arrived and killed her. But there were no signs of gunpowder residue on his hands. No gun has been found. He claims he didn't own one."

Asia stood to stretch her legs, "That's what bothering me. It's normal to look at the spouse or a loved one in cases like this, but this is going to be a hard case to bring to the grand jury. The evidence is circumstantial. I'm not sure why Brandon approved these charges."

Christine crossed her arms. "Family and friends have said on record that Lawrence and Janice weren't getting along. They said Janice had grown depressed. She filed for divorce two weeks prior to the murder. Maybe he was angry and didn't want to be stuck with paying her alimony. They'd been together ten years."

Asia paced the floor. "Do we know if either of them had been unfaithful?"

Christine shook her head. "Just rumors among her family. Lawrence was always away from the home at odd hours, but he denied having any affairs. He said it was the nature of his real estate business."

Asia looked at her assistant. "We need something that's going to convince the grand jury this guy needs to go on trial for murdering his wife. By the way, were you able to get the photos for me of Adam Locklear's crime scene?"

Christine appeared confused, "Yes, I have them. I thought Brandon wanted you to move away from the Locklear case."

Asia held out her hand. "Where are the photos? I need to do a comparison."

Christine nodded and went out the room. She returned with a folder. "These were sent over by the crime lab."

Asia took the folder and laid the contents next

to the photos of Janice Warren on her desk. "Come look at this so I'm not having a crazy moment here."

Christine stepped behind her desk to look at the photos. Her young assistant peered down for a few minutes. She finally turned to Asia, her eyes wide. "These look really similar."

"You agree with me, then? Whoever shot Janice Warren also shot Adam in a similar fashion. Straight to the head. I'm not into coincidences, but they're both in their office. Janice at her home office. Adam in his office."

"You're not trying to connect these two cases?"

"I'm not trying to on purpose, but my gut says something isn't right here. What we know is someone shot Warren's wife. Then someone shot Warren's lawyer. We want to convict this man of his wife's murder and the evidence is pretty circumstantial. We need to be digging in all related areas, no matter how crazy it may seem."

Christine nodded. "After you put it like that, it does seem weird."

Asia placed her hand on her hips and stared out the window for a moment. She took a breath. "Adam was representing Lawrence. As his lawyer, if he had something to prove his client's innocence, he would have to tell me."

"But this wasn't even your case yet. I mean Brandon hadn't assigned it yet."

"I know. But Adam thought the information he had needed to be told to me. Maybe he thought this was the kind of case Brandon would give me." She looked at Christine. "I need to know more about Janice Warren. What did she do exactly?"

"Well, she ran an online business. She managed a small group of virtual assistants."

"Find out about her clients. As a matter fact, dig further into both Janice and Lawrence's past. Did the Warrens have children?"

"No. They didn't have children. That could've been the source of her unhappiness."

Asia moved papers around on her desk. "True. I want to know about their past relationships."

Christine frowned. "Brandon wants us to pursue a grand jury in a few weeks. Isn't this moving away from proving Mr. Warren did it?"

Asia eyed her assistant. "This is about making sure we have a solid case to present. We can't let anything slip up on us. If we miss something, believe me, Brooke Cannon will make us look like idiots in the courtroom. I know you're heading out of town tomorrow afternoon for Thanksgiving with your folks in Florida, try to get as much of this to me as possible."

Christine nodded, "Will do. I hope you're taking some time off."

"There will be no missing Thursday's feast, but I will probably be working after that."

After Christine left her office, Asia pulled out a mug shot of Lawrence Warren. His face was scruffy, unlike the real estate brochure that was also inside the folder. On the front of the brochure, Warren was dressed in a sharp suit, standing with a wide smile outside a grand home in the background. A memory brushed against her mind, but before the thought fully formed she was interrupted by the phone.

She grabbed the phone, "Hello."

"Ms. Reed?"

"Yes, this is she."

"Hello, this is Dana Locklear."

"Yes, how are you doing?"

"My kids are here at the house. You mentioned letting you know about the memorial services for Adam. I will be having the service next Wednesday. Me and the kids just want to get through the holidays."

"I'm so sorry. I know this must be a tough time. Thank you for letting me know."

"Any news?"

"I'm afraid I don't have any news. Adam's case is a priority for Detective Coleman."

"Adam doesn't have any family and it would be good to get his body buried."

"I understand. We will keep you updated. I will be at the memorial services next week."

After Asia hung up the phone, she wondered who else would attend the services to say goodbye to Adam Locklear. She opened the real estate brochure not sure what she was looking for. Maybe they should dig deeper into Lawrence's financials. There had to be a much stronger motive for a successful real estate guy to kill his wife.

Her phone rang again, making Asia jump in her chair. "Hello."

"Ms. Reed, it's Detective Coleman. I think you may want to come see this. Adam Locklear's case just got more interesting."

"Really? Unfortunately, I'm supposed to steer clear of anything having to do with Adam. DA assigned me to Lawrence Warren's case."

"Well then, this will definitely interest you. This

notebook, or diary; really, that we found in Adam's safe. It belongs to Janice Warren."

Asia gripped the desk. Then she remembered to breathe. "I'll be right over." She hung up the phone, her mind whirling.

These cases really are connected.

Chapter 17

Tuesday, November 22 at 5:30 p.m.

Asia rubbed her head as she read through the highlighted passages from Janice Warren's diary.

He hit me over and over again. After he finished I lay on the floor for what seemed like hours, too scared to move.

Asia frowned and stared at Coleman. "Who is this guy? Is she saying Lawrence beat her? How did Adam get this diary?"

Coleman leaned back in his chair, clasping his hands behind his head, "As far as how Adam got the notebook I have two theories. Lawrence could have given it to him because he thought it would help his case. Or someone else passed the book to Adam."

Asia commented, "If it's Lawrence she's talking

about, this doesn't help his case. Who else was close enough to Janice to have access to something this personal?" She crossed her arms as though to brace herself for what Coleman would drop next.

"Candie Parker."

Asia raised her eyebrow. "They knew each other?"

"Candie and Janice were friends. They met when they were escort girls back in the day. This diary reads like a memoir. It's like Janice was recording her past. She mentions a woman named Candie early in the book. I have confirmed with Candie this morning that they were friends. Also, that argument that happened at the time Officer Lane walked in had to do with Brooke."

"Brooke Cannon?" Asia shook her head, "So it really was a jealousy thing going on? Not that that matters. I want to know if Candie was aware of this diary?"

"She says Janice never mentioned any of this to her. We're checking the diary for fingerprints to see if we can find others who may have had their hands on the notebook besides Janice and Adam."

Coleman shuffled the copied pages. "Janice mentions this guy in the highlighted entries quite a bit, but she doesn't name him."

"Why? Do you think she was going to try to publish this as a book?"

"It's possible. Someone could have found out. Maybe didn't want any secrets revealed. Could be a motive for why she was killed."

"Yeah, but are there really any major secrets? There is this guy who was pretty horrible to her. He was definitely violent. In this passage, he held a gun to her head." She looked down at the report Coleman handed her when she arrived earlier. "You know what really stood out to me the first time I looked at the crime scene for Janice was how similar it looked to Adam's. So, the gun used on Janice was the same caliber that killed Adam?"

Coleman nodded, "Yep. We're possibly looking at the same person. Adam had that notebook."

"Explains why the killer took his laptop and phone." Asia rubbed her hand across her forehead. This was almost too much to process. "Janice had to have this electronically stored in a cloud system somewhere, right? I'm assuming if she had plans to publish this it had to be transferred from this handwritten form."

"I agree. We're attempting to track down any electronic versions. We do have phone records that we're comparing for both of them. Adam's phone went dead that night. It's possible the assailant smashed it."

Asia sighed. "At least something is coming together. There was no camera footage around the Warren's home?"

"The Warrens had a security system, but get this, the day before she was killed, Janice requested more cameras be placed in the home."

"Was Lawrence Warren aware of this?"

"He claims he knows nothing about her request for further security. Remember they had been separated and he was living in an apartment."

Asia contemplated, "It's possible she wanted the security knowing she would have that big house to herself."

Coleman shrugged. "They lived in a gated community, actually not too far from Adam's home."

"Interesting. Someone or something spooked her. Did she mention any fears to anyone in her life?"

"No. If anything she'd become more withdrawn. People assumed she was depressed about the divorce." Coleman pointed to the copied passages from the diary. "This guy she writes about was a scary dude. I hate to say it, but it's not Lawrence. She clearly says she met Lawrence later. Read."

Asia scanned the passage.

It was hard to believe after so many years I would meet the man of my dreams. Lawrence is truly a kind and sweet man. I'm looking forward to our life together.

Wrong man. Those were Adam's words to her. "She names Lawrence. Even claims he's the man of her dreams. So why did their marriage fall apart?"

"It was a complete surprise to Lawrence."

"I'm not trying to bring an innocent man before the grand jury in a few weeks. We have to dig harder on who this guy could be in Janice's notebook. How does she end the relationship with him?"

Coleman picked up the last copied page. "Apparently, he was convicted of a crime. Not against her though. He was sentenced to prison."

"So we can look at who's recently been released around the time of Janice's murder? See if there's any connections."

Coleman asked, "Still, how would someone find out about Janice writing this diary? How would they know Adam had the book too? Candic didn't know about the notebook."

Asia looked at her phone. It was getting late.

"I guess we need to end this for the day. I'm due at my parent's home for Thanksgiving tomorrow. You have plans?"

Coleman stood and stretched. "Yes, my daughter and I usually head down to Columbia, South Carolina to visit with my wife's parents. Imani likes to spend the holidays with her maternal grandparents."

"I see. I'm sure it's good for her grandparents to see her, especially..."

"With their daughter in jail. Yes, I try to give them as much time with their granddaughter as possible. I do need to leave out and get rested for the drive tomorrow."

"Of course. We'll get back to who this mystery man is after the holidays. Just as long as we find something very soon."

"I wish we hadn't charged Lawrence, but all the evidence pointed towards him. A text was made to his phone from hers the night she was killed. He came to the house because she asked him to come. He could have easily gone over to the house in anger and shot her."

"You're right. But he didn't. Someone set him up. They killed Adam to further cover their tracks."

Chapter 18

Thursday, Thanksgiving – November 24

It was a day to celebrate and give thanks, but Asia found herself flitting from moments of self-pity to trying hard not to think about work. She rarely took days off and cherished holidays with her family. Today, she was finding it difficult to fully be present.

Jo and Bryan were in the happiest place she'd seen them. BJ was sitting in his dad's lap while Jo held Alisa. Across from them Toni leaned against her boyfriend, Cam. The young couple was beaming. Asia thought Cam would pop the question at any time. She wouldn't be surprised if her baby sister were walking down the aisle next year.

She glanced back where her parents sat with her

youngest brother. Probably the biggest surprise was her nerdy little brother brought a date this Thanksgiving. Only Toni, Cori's twin knew Cori had been dating a co-worker for several months.

Last time Asia brought anyone home was in high school and that was because she had to. Her boyfriends had to meet her dad before she went anywhere with them.

She slipped through the kitchen out the side door; she needed some air. It was in the fifties, but the sun shone bright on her parent's deck. Her long sweater and knit leggings felt good. She'd opted to leave the heels home today and wear her Skechers.

Asia sensed someone standing behind her. She glanced over her shoulder to see Jax grinning at her. She asked, "Aren't you going to catch the game with the rest of the guys?"

He rubbed his tummy. "I'm so full right now it's unreal. I needed some air. I knew Vanessa could cook, but she did that."

Asia had to smile despite being annoyed with Jax's presence. "Too bad I never picked up her cooking skills."

"Those skills are priceless. The way to a man's

heart is his stomach, but I haven't run across a woman yet that can throw a meal down like that."

"Is that all your criteria?"

He scoffed. "Those are the basics. What about you?"

Asia thought. "That's a good question."

"Oh, come on. All women know exactly what they want in a man."

"Apparently, I haven't figured that out yet. Maybe because I've run across some real scoundrels."

"I'm sure you will find someone."

"Aren't you being encouraging? What's going on with you?"

"We don't have to be at each other's throats, you know? I'm not your enemy."

"I know. Still, I don't think you came out here just for air. I remember you said you had something to tell me and Jo."

"I can always rely on you to not beat around the bush, Asia. You're right. I do have something to tell both of you. I guess I'll start with you. Depending how you handle it, at least I know Jo will handle it slightly better than you." He smiled.

Asia twisted her mouth. "I can't wait to hear."

"Well, you know I published a book last year

with S & E Publishers, and it became a New York Times bestseller."

"Yeah, I read it. True crime always offers an interesting read."

"Good to know you read it. I hope you like my next book. It's a work-in-progress now. My agent suggested the topic to me, and I have to say at first I wasn't too keen on it. But, I eventually decided to go for it."

Asia frowned. "It's still true crime?"

"Yes, except instead of an anthology of stories, this one will be a biography."

"Who are you writing about?"

"Someone you know."

Asia eyed him. "Who?"

"Jeffrey Maddock"

She stepped back. "You're serious?"

He shrugged. "It's a guaranteed bestseller."

Asia narrowed her eyes. "It also doesn't hurt that your sister arrested the man and your other sister was on the prosecution team."

Jax bowed his head. "I was hoping you weren't going to see it that way. I mean, don't you have questions about the man? What drives a person to turn into a serial killer?"

"Maddock is evil."

Jax raised his eyebrows. "Everyone has some evil floating around in them. Why did he have such an intense amount that made him want to kill?"

"I don't know. He doesn't deserve this kind of attention. He's a narcissist who got off on control and killing."

"Those women's family and friends, don't they have unanswered questions?"

"Come on, Jax. You know some things people do can't be explained. The best I can do for families and friends of a victim is to put the person behind bars so they don't hurt someone else. Ensure they receive punishment."

"Don't you ever wonder if we could stop people from doing horrible things if we knew the triggers?"

She rolled her eyes. "That's impossible to know. You're sounding like a movie I saw a few years ago with Tom Cruise."

Jax laughed. "I know the movie you're talking about. Minority Report. That's not what I'm getting at here. You can't control what a person does, but there has to be another way of switching their mindset."

"Yeah, they need a morality check. A healthy fear of God."

"I'm not going to argue with you, but life can be unfair, clouding people's judgement."

Asia rolled her eyes, "No doubt Maddock was a mental case. He used his real estate practice to lure woman into a date where he ultimately murdered them. The women all happened to look very similar to his abusive mother. He was caught and sentenced to life. End of story."

"There's more to his story. I've been finding out some interesting things about Maddock. Things you and Jo may not have known."

Asia looked at him. "Like what?"

"I bet you didn't know him and his lawyer were friends growing up?"

It took her a few seconds to process what Jax said. Asia shook her head. "Locklear and Maddock grew up together? How did you find out that?"

"I've been an investigative reporter for fifteen years, specializing in crime. I have my ways. But yeah, apparently when Maddock was looking for a lawyer, no one really wanted to touch his case. I mean he practically confessed. According to my source, Locklear had to come through for his buddy. He owed him."

He owed him. "For what?"

"That's one of the things on my list to find out.

Especially with Locklear getting killed, which I'm sure you've heard all about."

Asia crossed her arms. She was sure Jax knew nothing about her brief relationship with Adam. She pondered out loud. "I always wondered why Locklear took his case. He tried to make Maddock look like he was some kind of victim because of his mom's abuse. I'm just glad the jury didn't fall for it."

Jax reiterated, "Look, the guy's clearly crazy."

Asia shook her head. "He deserves to be behind bars. He wasn't insane. He knew exactly what he was doing."

"Maddock really got under your skin. I guess he did to Jo too." He looked behind him. "Is she ever going back to Homicide?"

"Jo's enjoying motherhood."

"What about you?"

"What about me?"

"You seem to love your career, but don't you want a family?"

"I could ask you the same question."

Jax swallowed. "I've been thinking about it since my mom died. I feel like I kind of need to have a legacy. That's one of the reasons I started writing books."

Asia thought for a moment. "You're blessed you found another career. I haven't been liking mine too much lately." She thought about Locklear. The entire time she dated him, she didn't have a clue about his background. When Maddock's trial rolled around, she had long parted ways with Locklear.

She wasn't happy that Jax wanted to write a book about Maddock, but for once, the brother she had trouble accepting proved to be the nudge she needed to dig a little deeper.

There was something she was missing from Adam's past.

Chapter 19

Wednesday, November 30 at 3:33 p.m.

Quite a few people attended Adam's memorial service. Asia stopped counting at fifty heads. At least fifty people meant Adam wasn't all that bad. She looked over to see Detective Coleman also observing the crowd. She couldn't resist noticing how well his suit fit.

Behave, Asia!

She walked over to the detective. "Nice turn out."

Coleman shook his head. "So, what are you thinking, Counselor? Could anyone in this room be Adam's killer?"

"Killers often like to see the results of their wrongdoing." Asia let her eyes wander around the room. She recognized other lawyers, as well as a few people she was sure were Adam's clients. Many were giving condolence to the family. Asia turned to Coleman, "I'm going to talk to Dana and meet Adam's kids."

She walked up to Dana who stood beside her two teens. "Ms. Reed, it's good to see you. I don't know if you've met Adam's children. This is Dallas. He will be off to college next fall and Justine is a rising high school junior."

Asia shook the teenagers' hands. "I'm sorry for your loss. Your dad and I were on the opposite ends in the courtroom, but I considered him a friend. He was a phenomenal person to have in your corner."

Dallas, who looked like a younger version of Adam though not as tall, responded. "Thank you, Ms. Reed. That's kind of you."

Asia stepped closer to Dana so she could quietly talk to her. "Do you know most of these people? Would you say they were Adam's friends?"

Dana closed her eyes, "I used to attend events with Adam early in our marriage, but I stopped when the kids were young. I can't tell you if these people were really Adam's friends or not."

"Do you remember a Janice Warren?"

"Janice? I knew a person named Janice, but not

sure if her last name was Warren? She was a client of Adam's, I think. Long time ago."

Asia turned to see what had caught Dana's attention. Candie Parker was standing at the door.

"I guess I should have known she would be here." Dana turned towards her children as though she was protecting them.

Adam definitely made a lasting impression with the women in his life.

She took a deep breath and approached Candie. "Candie, I don't know if you remember me."

Candie's eyes widened as if she felt cornered. "Yes, I remember you, Ms. Reed."

Asia glanced over her shoulder. "You mind walking with me for a bit?"

Candie looked unsure. "Sure."

They walked outside the room where the memorial service had been held, passing a larger-than-life portrait of Adam. It was a fairly recent photo capturing the crinkles that had grown around his eyes from age. Asia commented, "He was a very handsome man. I understood you knew Adam a long time, long before you started working for him."

"I met him through a mutual friend. He encouraged me to continue my paralegal courses and said if I finished, he would have a job for me. He didn't break his promise. He was a good boss and, as crazy as it may seem, a friend."

Asia stopped walking, "You didn't like Brooke Cannon coming around though?"

Candie raised her eyebrow. "That's because she wasn't good for him. Her whole family is bad news."

"You told the police Brooke came by the Monday before Adam's death. Are you sure? She claimed she hadn't seen him in weeks."

Candie's nose flared. "She lied. In fact, I could tell she was very angry. She stomped through the doors, ignoring me, and barged into Adam's office. Adam told me to head home and closed the door, but I heard her screaming."

"About what? Why didn't you mention this to the police?"

"What do you mean? I did tell them she came by."

"But you neglected to mention the argument was heated. Did you hear anything?"

She nodded. "She kept saying to him, how could you betray me like that?"

Betray. What had Adam done to Brooke?

Candie asked, "Are you guys any closer to finding out who did this?"

"I'm afraid not. There's a lot of unanswered questions. Especially about the days leading up to Adam's death. Wednesday afternoon, Officer Lane stopped by. Do you remember?"

"Yes. He came to ask questions, I guess. Clear up his account."

"How were things with you and Adam the last day?"

"What do you mean?"

"You said you were friends? You knew him well. Did you two have words about anything?"

Candie wilted. "I was heated with him. I told him I didn't know why he was wasting his time with Brooke Cannon. She'd left a rude message for him to call her." Candie squeezed her hands, "After Officer Lane left, I asked Adam what was going on. He told me not worry." Candie's mouth quivered and turned away, "When I left, I had this feeling he was hiding something really bad."

Asia faced Candie. "You seem to be really hostile about Brooke Cannon. You sure this isn't a jealousy thing?"

Candie snapped, "I'm not jealous. Years ago, Adam helped my friend, Janice. She was struggling to get out of a really bad relationship. Adam figured out a way to get her *problem*... removed. At least for a while. He had to leave Cannon Law Firm after that."

Asia asked, "Did he leave on his own or was he threatened?"

"He left on his own before anyone really found out what he did to help Janice."

"Don't keep me in suspense, Candie. Does this have to do with Adam being killed?"

She shook her head, "I don't know. I've been wondering. The guy Adam helped get put away was practically torturing Janice. I remembered her trying to hide the bruises. She wouldn't leave him, no matter how hard I begged."

Asia wanted to strangle Candie. "Who was the guy?"

Candie stared at her and whispered. "Payton. Payton Cannon."

Asia thought back to her visit to Brooke's office. "Payton Cannon. Brooke's older brother?"

Candie shook her head.

Asia could see Candie was visibly trembling. She spoke softly, "Why didn't you say something before now?"

"It didn't occur to me. Not until the detective

mentioned Janice had a diary. She never mentioned anything to me about the diary, but then I remembered she used to go to therapy. I figured she must have been writing things down from the past. Then I started thinking, why was Brooke Cannon suddenly coming around so much. Why was she angry at Adam? Maybe she found out what Adam did."

What had Adam done to Payton Cannon?

Both Asia and Candie looked startled as the elevators opened. The woman who was the center of their conversation stepped out.

"I have to go check on my son." Candie hurried away.

Asia noticed Brooke wasn't alone. An older man strutted beside her with a cane in his hand. She guessed this man had to be the one and only Preston Cannon.

"Hello, Brooke."

Brooke wiped her tear-stained face appearing shaken. She produced a faint smile. "Asia, how are you? Of course you would be here. Adam was dear to you too. Father, you know Asia Reed. She's the daughter of our former Chief of Police."

"Yes, I know you." The older man's voice

boomed. "I'm sure your father is proud. I believe all of you are in law enforcement in some capacity?"

Asia nodded. "Yes, we're affectionately known as the crime-fighting family."

Brooke smiled. "Asia is quite the formidable opponent, Father. I will be seeing her in the courtroom in the near future."

Asia smiled, "Grand jury selection is coming up soon. It's good Mr. Warren found you, especially after losing Adam as his lawyer. That must have been devastating for him."

Brooke rubbed her lips together. "Yes, it was."

Preston spoke up for his daughter. "Devastating to all of us. Adam was like a son to me. I taught Adam and my daughter everything I knew." He grinned, "Mr. Warren won't be without a strong defense. It will be on you," he pointed towards her, "Ms. Reed, to prove his guilt."

Asia felt a fighting spirit sneak up her belly. That spark she felt right before she delivered a blow with her closing argument. "Oh, I plan to, Mr. Cannon."

She watched the Cannons as they entered the room.

Coleman slipped past them and headed towards her. He gave her a weary look. "Not sure I like that look on your face. Someone bothered you."

Asia nodded, "I'm very bothered, but in a good way. I think we have our killer's name."

Chapter 20

Wednesday, November 30 at 5:17 p.m.

Asia followed Isaac back to the precinct. She wanted to know as much about Payton Cannon as possible. They needed a solid theory for her to bring to her boss in the morning. Being the DA, Brandon would not take too kindly to her suddenly finding another suspect after he'd instructed her to prepare for the grand jury in a few weeks.

When they arrived, Lamb was sitting at his desk. Asia noticed for the first time the older detective had a smile on his face.

"What's got you so happy, partner?" Coleman asked.

"I'm just smiling over how justice prevails." He

pointed at Asia. "Your buddy Adam kicks the dust and so does one of his former clients."

Asia and Coleman both blurted out, "What?"

Lamb spins his computer monitor around. "Ethan Consentino. I had no idea somebody finally put that scumbag away. Looks like he didn't last but eight months in prison. Somebody shanked him at Central. He got life, but somebody took it."

Coleman nodded, "Justice prevails. Now if we could track down Payton Cannon."

Lamb grimaced, "Payton Cannon. Preston Cannon's son?"

"Yes." Asia stared at Lamb. "You know about him?"

"Yeah, he was one of those ones I was glad to see put away. It wasn't my case, but I remember Payton got mad one night and beat the owner of a bar almost to death. His dad couldn't get him out of that one. If I'm not mistaken Locklear ended up getting some kind of deal for Payton on a lesser charge of manslaughter instead of attempted second-degree murder. Daddy Cannon must not have been happy because Locklear set up his own practice not too long after that."

Asia frowned. "That explains any animosity towards Adam." She stared at Lamb, "You know he was involved with Janice Warren. He used to beat her up pretty bad."

Lamb's mouth hung open for a minute. "Well, I'll be. I never made the connection. Actually, now that I think about it. The guy Payton beat up, I believe it was over a woman."

Asia stepped forward, "Well, those feelings may have festered over the years. We don't think Lawrence Warren killed his wife. If Payton had some type of deal, he may have been recently released."

"On it." Coleman blurted. "Here, he was released on September 16th. His parole officer is Randy Lewis. I can call and check with him to see when's the last time he touched based with him."

Asia leaned over to view the mugshot on Coleman's screen. "I've seen him."

"The day I visited Brooke Cannon. That guy showed up at her office. He was wearing these thick glasses, but that's him." She thought for a moment. "I wonder if he had a habit of messing with his appearance. He managed to slip out of the building undetected. That has always bothered me."

Coleman nodded, "I've thought about that too. It's possible he could have slipped out under our noses, maybe posing as an officer."

Asia grabbed her purse. "That sounds plausible. He's definitely a planner. We need his address. Also, we might want to see what judge can sign off on a search warrant ASAP. If Payton is our guy, and he used his gun twice, what are the chances he still has it in his possession?"

"Good point." Coleman frowned, "Where are you rushing off too?"

"To pay Brooke Cannon a visit."

Coleman stood and waved his hands. "Woah! Is that really wise to do? The guy we're looking for is her brother. She doesn't need to be tipping him off."

"I have no intentions of alerting Brooke. I do need her to know I intend to ask the DA to drop the charges against her client Lawrence Warren."

"Yeah, but won't that still tip her a bit? Suppose she knows her brother committed these killings. She could be helping him hide out."

"I didn't get the impression Brooke was that close to her brother. She values her reputation. You work on locating Payton."

As Asia walked out, what she didn't say to Coleman was at the memorial service she saw a woman unraveling. *Were Brooke's tears really just for*

Adam or was the supposed friend carrying around a burdensome secret?

It was time for another woman-to-woman talk.

Chapter 21

Wednesday, November 30 at 6:09 p.m.

Asia tapped on the door of Cannon Law Firm. She cupped her face against the glass window. While the front of the offices looked dark, she could see lights towards the back. Asia felt pretty sure Brooke would've returned to her office.

Suddenly the lights lit up in the alcove, and Brooke appeared. Asia stepped from the door and waited for it to open.

Brook peeked out, "Asia? What are you doing here?"

"I needed to speak with you. I figured you would've headed back to the office after the memorial."

"Us workaholics do think alike, but really, this isn't a good time."

"Well, I might save you some work. I have some information that could affect one of your clients facing a grand jury in a few weeks."

Brooke blinked. "Couldn't you have called me on the phone?"

"This was better in person, plus I was in the neighborhood." Asia cringed inside at that statement and was suddenly doubtful of why she'd come to see Brooke.

For a moment, Asia wasn't sure if Brooke was going to let her in. She pulled the door wide open so Asia could slip through.

As she entered, she noticed the secretary wasn't in. "Did you send Ms. Bishop home early?"

"Yes. She would try to hang with me, but I needed to be alone." Brooke cleared her throat. "What is it you have to tell me? It's been a long day. I probably should have gone home after Adam's memorial. That was more emotional than I thought it would be."

"I'm sorry. I wanted to let you know I'm talking to the DA in the morning about dropping the Lawrence Warren case."

Brooke's face froze, "Why?"

"I have reason to believe Mr. Warren didn't kill his wife."

Brooke crossed her arms as if a cold draft had drifted around her. "The DA's office had a pretty solid case against Mr. Warren. This is surprising."

Asia stared at Brooke. "You don't sound happy for your client, Brooke. I mean I know not being in the courtroom is a loss, but there will be other times."

Brooke smiled, but her eyes remained haunted. "I'm sorry. Like I said it's been a long day. If you can convince the DA to drop the charges, I know my client will be..." Asia noticed Brooke's eyes flicker past her. "...very happy."

Brooke's voice dipped so low Asia could barely hear her. Her own stomach started to churn, and Asia sensed movement from behind her.

They weren't alone.

Asia spun around to see Payton Cannon stepping from Brooke's office.

She turned back to Brooke who looked frozen in place. "I'm sorry. I didn't realize you had a *client*."

"Oh, I'm not a client." Payton stepped forward. He held out his hand. "I'm her brother. Payton Cannon."

Asia looked at the man's hand. She reached for his hand, realizing she needed to keep her cool. "Nice to meet you. I met your father earlier at

Adam's memorial. Who knew I would meet your family today, Brooke?"

"I remember seeing you at the memorial." Payton commented.

Asia nodded. "I don't remember seeing you. Were you and Adam friends? I know he worked here at Cannon for a number of years."

The corner of Payton's mouth tugged as if his lip was trying to downturn away from the smile plastered on his face. "Adam and I were friends at one time. Long time ago. Shame to lose him so...violently. My dad thought the world of Adam." Payton chuckled, "I think he would've preferred to have Adam as a son."

Payton looked over at his sister. "I really stopped liking Adam when he rejected my sister. Look at her, she's so beautiful and smart. Dad's favorite. It devastated her when Adam married that woman."

Asia felt like something crawled down her back and arms. For a moment, she felt as paralyzed as Brooke appeared. She remembered to breathe. "I'm sorry to hear that. Adam wasn't liked by a lot of people. I apologize for disturbing you both. I'll be in touch tomorrow, Brooke."

Brooke's eyes flickered towards her as if to say, "Get out now."

Asia moved towards the door.

"I heard you were dropping the charges against the Warren guy. Why?"

She turned, thinking she really should've listened to Coleman. *What exactly did I think I was going to accomplish again?*

Asia prayed, *Lord, help me get away from this psychopath.*

She crossed her arms, "There wasn't enough evidence. Your sister is Warren's attorney. I'm sure she would agree."

Payton stared. "I know Brooke would agree. She knew Warren didn't kill Janie."

Janie. Asia glanced over at Brooke whose face had become flushed. Brooke started to shake her head slowly as if to warn her brother to stop talking.

Asia continued praying. It occurred to her this man knew exactly what was going on and her trying to pretend ignorance may not work in her favor.

Payton stared at her directly. "Janie didn't deserve to have her life taken like that. Warren knew she moved on to someone else and he wanted to stop her."

Warren? Did he mean himself?

Asia concentrated on keeping her thoughts from affecting her face and her movements, which was not easy. She had no recollection of feeling this kind of fear before. It didn't help that she wasn't sure if Payton had moved closer or if he just seemed larger than he did a few minutes ago.

He smiled, his pearly white teeth perfect. The man looked more like an elite, Ivy League man than a hardened criminal who just got out of jail a few months ago. "Brooke, I think your friend here forgot to tell you something."

Asia frowned, "What would that be, Mr. Cannon?"

He slipped his hand behind his back and pulled out a gun. "That you want me. Only one problem. I'm not going back to jail."

Brooke barked, "No." She held her hands up, "What are you doing?"

Asia shook her head. "I think you should listen to your sister. I came here to share my recommendations for one of her clients."

He laughed. "And I just got a very frantic phone call from my parole officer. Apparently, the police are looking for me."

Asia took a breath. "If you haven't done anything, then you have nothing to fear."

"We both know I've been busy."

Brooke whimpered.

"Stop your whining, little sister." Payton snapped. He waved the gun around. "I should have never been sent to prison. That guy they *claimed* I assaulted deserved what he got."

Tears ran down Brooke's face. "Why can't you just go?"

"Go? I thought you missed your brother." Payton drawled.

As the brother and sister talked, Asia inched her way backwards. She was less than ten feet from the door. But this man had shot two people point blank in the head.

Can I really make a run for it?

It could have been her wishful thinking, but Asia heard police sirens in the distance. She looked at Payton. "Do you really think it's wise to stay around here?"

He pointed the gun at her, "You're right. I should really get out of here and take you with me. Or better yet, just get rid of you. Sister, you can clean this one up."

Brooke screamed, "No."

Asia held her hands up in front of her.

Lord, take me to you.

Chapter 22

Wednesday, November 30 at 7:01 p.m.

Asia's body slammed onto the floor. She wasn't sure if she was hit, but felt something crash into her ribs. She laid still hearing sirens so close they had to be outside the offices.

Asia looked down to see that Brooke had fallen across her. She whispered, "Brooke." The woman's eyes stared at her for an instant and then life seemed to fade away.

Asia knew that bullet was really for her. She looked up. Payton stared out the window, blue lights bounced off his face. He glanced down where his sister lay. There was a brief look of remorse, but it disappeared as he turned his attention to Asia.

He raised the gun.

Asia closed her eyes, praying in earnest.

The door behind her burst open and she heard shouting from what seemed like all directions. She held her hands over her head at the sound of gunfire, bracing her body to be hit at any moment.

Someone moved the weight of Brooke's body off her. "Asia, are you hurt?"

Was that Coleman's voice? She opened her eyes. Her voice seemed stuck in her throat.

"Let's get you out of here." Coleman pulled her to her feet. She stumbled forward, but he caught her and held her close.

She turned her head and saw Brooke on the floor, a bloody gash in her crisp white shirt. There were no signs of life.

Payton had slipped down the secretary's desk to the floor with a gunshot wound to his head.

She asked, "Who shot him?"

"Don't worry about that. Let's get you checked out." Coleman took off her blood-soaked coat and placed his coat around her before leading her outside.

Asia stood outside for a while before an ambulance arrived. "I'm fine," she insisted.

Coleman rubbed her arm, "We can go into all the details later. Let them check you out."

Asia lay in the hospital bed surrounded by her mother, Toni and Jo. "I'm fine; I told you. Just bruising and..." Asia held up her shaky hands. "My nerves are shot."

Her mother grabbed her hands. "I'm so glad God protected you. You..." she looked around at all her girls. "All of you have managed to scare me to pieces now."

Toni smiled and rubbed her mom's arm. "We can't fight crime, Mom, without running into evil."

Jo nodded. "So sorry about Brooke Cannon."

"Me too. I don't know why she threw herself in front of me. That bullet was meant for me."

There was a knock at the door. Asia looked up to see Isaac. "Detective Coleman?"

"Sorry to interrupt, I can come back."

Toni spoke, "Oh no. Please come in, Detective. We'll leave."

Asia saw her sisters share a wink as they led their mom outside into the hospital hallway.

Coleman smiled, "You have a great family."

"Thanks, I really needed to see their faces. So, what have you got for me?"

"Basically, your instincts were on target about Adam's past. He probably found out Payton had been released and was responsible for Janice's death. He may have even known Payton would eventually come after him."

Asia shook his head. "Why didn't Adam warn me sooner?"

Coleman shrugged. "Maybe he was trying to figure out what to do. We checked his deliveries and Locklear received a package that Monday before he died. We think the notebook was delivered to him posthumously by Janice. He was still her lawyer."

"So, Payton had probably returned to torturing Janice. I wish she would have told someone. How did Payton know or did he know about the notebook?"

"We think Locklear may have said too much to Brooke. Remember the argument that Monday night? Brooke may have given Payton some ammunition. This links back to him."

"You know, I think in the end Brooke really wanted to do the right thing. She was torn between helping her brother, but she knew he was a monster too. I think Adam's death hit her hard. When I went to talk to her that first time she even hinted to me that Adam had hidden something away."

"She was supposedly in love with the guy. She

could have saved us a lot of trouble once she knew what her brother had done though. I mean was she really going to defend Lawrence Warren knowing he was innocent?"

"She may have thought her skills would keep him out of jail." Asia sighed. "Hey, by the way, I heard you got in the shot that took out Payton."

Coleman looked at her, "Just doing my job." He bowed his head. "I couldn't let him take you out, Counselor. We just got to know each other."

For the first time in several hours, Asia smiled. "I look forward to getting to know you better too, Detective."

Epilogue

Ten weeks later, February 14, 6:30 pm

Asia looked at herself in the mirror. She turned from side-to-side to ensure her close-fitting red dress fit smoothly. Spanx was her friend tonight thanks to many months of not working out.

It had been a brutal few months in the aftermath of Payton and Brooke's death. Preston Cannon briefly made an appearance on camera, but had since become a bit of a recluse with the loss of both of his adult children.

Asia took some much-needed time from work. Though she was back now, she still had trouble sleeping at night. Jo told her she was suffering from PTSD and should talk to someone. For now, Asia chose to make a commitment to Sunday service and started attending Wednesday night bible study with her mom. She was grateful to have her life and wanted more than her career to be her sole purpose for getting up in the morning.

She leaned over and applied the red lipstick to her lips. Tonight, instead of her usual ponytail, she let her long hair lay across her shoulders. It was a special occasion. She may be turning forty this year, but she had every intention of living outside her work.

The doorbell rang. Asia grabbed one more look at herself before heading towards the front door. She opened the door and grinned.

Isaac Coleman stood with a dozen red roses in his hand. "I hope this is appropriate." He offered her the bouquet.

She smiled. "I don't even remember the last time I received roses. These are very special. Let me put them in water before we go. Come on in."

Isaac followed her into the living room. "Feel free to have a seat."

He nodded, but turned his attention to the paintings on the wall.

Asia grabbed a vase from under the cabinet and filled it with water. She placed the vase on the counter and observed Isaac from the kitchen. Her hands were shaky as she arranged the roses inside the vase. She still wanted to pinch herself that she was actually doing this.

It was their third date and it just happened to be Valentine's Day. The first time Isaac asked her out was New Year's Eve. At the time, she'd told him she needed to see what her family was planning. Her mom, Jo and Toni fixed that and told her to bring him. So, she invited him and Imani to her parent's home. Her nerves were about to burst that night and tonight wasn't any easier.

She liked him. Really liked him. Her and Imani got along. She was thankful and prayed her thanks to God. Still in the back of her mind, she was scared.

Asia walked over to Isaac. He turned and she felt his eyes assessing her outfit.

"You look beautiful."

"Thank you."

"Are these paintings supposed to be you?"

She laughed. "Sort of. Toni called these the Diva series and I believe I was her inspiration."

"Well, I'm honored you would give me a chance."

Asia blinked, "What? Why wouldn't I?"

"I'm a single dad with a teenage daughter. My life is complicated."

"I don't think I have room to talk, Detective. I've completely missed out on life. Right now, I really want to live and share that experience with someone else. I can't think of anyone better."

Isaac returned a smile that warmed her heart. "Shall we?"

"Sure, let's go."

Before they reached the door, he asked, "Do you mind?"

Asia inquired, "What?"

Isaac leaned in and placed his arm around her waist. He lifted her chin and kissed her lightly on the cheek. "Happy Valentine's Day. I hope we have many more of these together."

Asia exclaimed, "I do too."

About the Author

Tyora Moody is the author Soul-Searching Suspense novels in the Reed Family Series, Eugeena Patterson Mysteries, Serena Manchester Series, and the Victory Gospel Series. She is also the author of the nonfiction book, *The Literary Entrepreneur's Toolkit*, and the compilation editor for the Stepping Into Victory Compilations under her company, Tymm Publishing LLC.

To contact Tyora about book club discussions or for book marketing workshops, visit her online at TyoraMoody.com.

Books by Tyora Moody

REED FAMILY SERIES

Relentless Heart, Book 3 (this book)
Troubled Heart, Book 2
Broken Heart, Book 1

EUGEENA PATTERSON MYSTERIES
Oven Baked Secrets, Book 2
Deep Fried Trouble, Book 1
Shattered Dreams: A Short Story

SERENA MANCHESTER SERIES
Hostile Eyewitness, Book 1

VICTORY GOSPEL SERIES
When Perfection Fails, Book 3
When Memories Fade, Book 2
When Rain Falls, Book 1